XEMU PULLED
MY FINGER

Joel Miller

Albion Entertainment Inc.

Dedicated to the they them in all of us

BOOK 1

THE PRESENT

At the end of the day... The hell with lemmings. Dodgy little fuckers they are.

No, that's not how I want to start all this off. Let's do this again. That's probably a really rude way to start a book. I think any story can begin better than that. Or maybe I should say I'm better than that. I'm not though. Either way, to clarify, I don't hate literal lemmings as a species. What I'm trying to do is make a philosophical statement.

How about this? At the beginning of the day, I'm tired of being a lemming. Yeah, that's what I'm trying to say. That sounds better for sure.

I had begun telling myself these very words every day for a while now and swore I'd continue to do so until something in my life changed. We, as an international being, had become tired of Earth's air. Tainted oxygen was one of the few things earthlings now agreed upon.

Lemmings, we had all started wearing masks to protect ourselves from that oxygen. For 2.4 billion years, since an event known as the Great Oxidation Event, Earth and Oxygen had been pals. Things had changed in the last year, though, and now good ol' oxygen was scary to us.

The situation had taken the metaphorical wind out of my sails, and I had taken refuge locked up within the walls of my house. It was now just the safe air within my house and me.

I no longer wanted to leave to see masked people walking down the street by themselves, people driving by themselves with a face shield on, walking into restaurants with a mask on but then taking it off to then eat, and all the other madness that had taken over my happy world. I wasn't sure if the air in my house was truly safer than the outside air, but it sure seemed to be. My health seemed fine. In turn, I thanked the heavens for my safe house air daily.

My house, or what I preferred to call my sexy air shrine, was a one-bedroom, one-bathroom, one coffee-maker, and one refrigerator haven. One day I had hoped to be able to afford a second refrigerator to keep my beers cold. Not to brag, but I was sure I was on my way.

Locked in my sexy air shrine for most of the day and night, I began to study. At first my "research" began with David Letterman interviews on Youtube. I think everyone's research on anything really should start with Letterman. In between the interviews, I'd rest my eyes and watch American-made pornography. I have always preferred foreign films, but America has always made the best porn, hands down. This Letterman/porn routine lasted a few short months and then unfortunately my life began to dull again. I was now tired of people, non-safe air, Letterman, and I hated to admit to it, but American-made porn even.

Transitioning, I began to read books. Oh, before we get into that I don't want to confuse you when I say transitioning, I don't mean changing my tiggly bits around; I meant it had been a long time since I had read an actual book and that's what I started to do next.

One wouldn't think I had a lot of books in my house. But I most certainly did. I had lots of books and boy did they have a lot of words in them. The issue, if anyone does have an issue, was the books were all written by The Church of Science & Celebrities & Stuff, or the CSCS. Members of the CSCS were known as CSters. CSters are not to be confused with people who like to take an afternoon nap. It should be noted that CSters are very committed to the CSCS and are in turn very well versed in the large catalog of scriptures and doctrines housed amongst its followers.

Muslims look towards Mecca. Christians look up. CSters they look at all. Science, celebrities, and of course "stuff." It was the combination of these three crucial branches that gave sense to CSters in an illogical Hollywood world. So, what was the last branch all about? What was the stuff? Well, stuff was most certainly not up for discussion. It was all very top secret. Since CSters were all very strong in knowledge, I had hopes of finding one of their grand poohbahs and asking if God was in fact happy because there was no Mrs. God. I had a strong feeling that a poo CSter would know the answer. I even had suspicions that this very question may have been the starting point, the focal point even, of the third branch of the CSCS. It may have been the stuff dreams were made of. [Please note, I apologize to Carly Simon for referencing her song here, "The Stuff That Dreams Are Made Of." But well... she's great, the song kicks ass, and it fit nicely. To clarify, the reference had nothing to do with *The Maltese Falcon* or Shakespeare for you smarty pants people.]

I had come to surmise that the hired CSCS writers were the Charles Dickens' of our day. They too must have been paid per word. The books are all really, really long. Now, I'll be honest. I didn't read too many of the words in those books. I don't consider myself lazy, but there were just a lot of them. All the reading would be too big of a commitment for even a pedophile. Oh, oops, bibliophile. I should really look words up on the internet before jotting them down in my story. I love the internet for that very reason. All the information is easily accessible and correct.

CHAPTER 2

C'est la vie

I did, however, start to like what I was able to read. If Tom Cruise was a CSter, maybe there was something to this religion thing after all. Tom Cruise had done lots of neat stuff. I know what you're thinking. "Well, maybe in movies! But that's not a gauge on how cool he is in real life." I'll tell you this naysayer, that is not necessarily true. How big is the WWE wrestling audience who think it's all fake? The answer is real, but in reality, I don't need to tell you it's all obviously quite real. Therefore, Tom Cruise is just as cool in real life as he is in his movies. I don't mean to pull the science card, but there are many science-driven people among us who like to make things difficult. So, to keep them entertained, sometimes you need "scientific facts" to prove those things. If we have to bring this subject up again later to save time and reduce word count, I'll just write Tom Cruise = WWE. You science-driven people will then know what I'm talking about.

So, if Tom Cruise was my male CSCS role model; It would be Juliette Lewis I'd choose to be my female CSCS role model. Truthfully, it was an easy decision after doing a Google search for the "top ten sexiest CSters on the planet." I had looked that up after trying to see if I could find "topless women deep sea fishing." A fun fact – if you change the spelling of amateur to amature you get a whole new list of topless women fishing. Why topless women deep sea fishing? Well, because I like to party. That's why.

CHAPTER 3

The "Show-Me" State

How did this horde of Church of Science & Celebrities & Stuff awesomeness find itself in my possession, you ask? OK, I know you didn't ask. As soon as anyone mentions the CSCS the room always goes quiet. Oh yeah, that happens here in Los Angeles too. It's not just a rest-of-the-world thing. I'm going to fill you in on my little conquest anyhow. There is of course a whole story to it.

Before the time of the mask, I had befriended a local barfly named Mary Sue. Mary Sue was cute as a button. Like Jean Harlow she had come to Los Angeles from America's Midwest. Missouri to be exact. Mary Sue had moved to Los Angeles not too many years before to become an actress. She told her family that she was going to "take the city by storm." And it could be argued she did.

Let me further explain what her personal city-storming conquest involved. While trooping through parties in the Hollywood Hills she had developed a slight cocaine problem. These things happen. For Mary Sue though the "problem" might have actually been a hereditary one. You see, many years earlier her mother had come to Hollywood to become an actress, take the city by storm as well, but most importantly for our story frequent the famous Playboy Mansion.

Her mom's storm was much like that of a tornado; her impact was clear, but she eventually disappeared, and life continued on. To say she "stormed" the Playboy Mansion would be much like the Trump supporters who had stormed, or many would argue rioted, the Capitol Building in the great year of 2021. 2021, it should be noted, was part of the year of the mask and so things were a bit nutty.

Mary Sue's mother bombarded the Playboy Mansion wearing odd hats made of various animal pelts and lots of makeup. Some may say not enough pelt and too much makeup even. She liked wearing the pelts as a tribute to her Missouri roots. She too, like the 2021 head rioter fella, often went shirtless. It was a different time, but like those Capitol Building angry people, she too ended up behind bars. It was not for storming, or again some may say rioting, the Playboy Mansion or the Capitol Building for that matter but instead for what the law called "indecent exposure." It should be noted If you are going to get arrested for indecent exposure it's better to do that on a Hollywood street corner. It just makes for a better story. It was nonsensical to her that she got arrested while real hookers were but a few short feet away, but sometimes that is how the dice roll. Eventually, Mary Sue's mother would see the ordeal that way too.

While in jail Mary Sue's mother had time to think, and she spent a lot of that time thinking about the Los Angeles hookers. She wondered if it would make more sense in condom commercials to have a guy having sex with a bunch of hookers instead of a happy couple smiling with a Trojan condom in hand? Hookers would get the message across a bit better, she told her cell-mates. Determined to make a difference, she left Los Angeles and moved back to Missouri to make condoms. When one of her condoms failed, Mary Sue was born. At least that's the story Mary Sue told people.

CHAPTER 4

Bert, Pimpin' the Plastic

It had been some time, decades to be exact, and the Playboy Mansion had since closed up shop. Hugh had popped off and so instead of meeting some old horny fella there, as her coked-out topless mother had done decades earlier, Mary Sue had met a new kind of fella at the CSCS. Her beau was a nice enough man who even came with his own walker. New shiny tennis balls at the tips and all.

Bert had made millions working as a plastic surgeon. Mary Sue was convinced that through a snip snip here and a snip snip there... here a snip... there a snip... everywhere a snip snip... she'd get that perfect Hollywood part one day. I wasn't completely unsure that she already hadn't.

Bert had dated a number of Mary Sue's throughout his many years. He may have even dated her mother at one point. While we'd sometimes joke about it, I was unsure if Bert would remember even if he had. I would wonder what would change in their relationship if they had found out Bert was actually Mary Sue's father. That would have thrown a wrench in things! Don't you think? Well, I'd like to hope it would have at least.

I would guess that Bert was in his eighties. He was tall and slender. His hair wasn't dyed but instead, he had opted for implants at some point. He was always clean-shaven and never left the house wearing anything other than a dress shirt and perfectly pressed slacks. He had a perfect set of fake teeth, and being that he was a plastic surgeon, there wasn't a wrinkle on his face to be seen.

I assumed plastic surgeons traded out plastic surgery services, because it only makes sense that you can't do plastic surgery on your own face. Bert and all of his plastic surgeon old man friends had that perfect robot looking smile. Why there were no plastic surgeon women in his circle I didn't understand.

Bert enjoyed sitting with us outside at the wine bar. I didn't like sitting outside drinking wine much, it made me feel like a wino with a table. Though not often, on occasion, Bert would accompany us, and I'd make do. However, if we opted to go to a different bar, he would never join us. I think it was because the wine bar was easily accessible and close to his home.

So, knowing all of this, on occasion Mary Sue and I would go to other places to make sure Bert wouldn't be around. In that endeavor, the endeavor of being fully respectful to Bert of course, I'll be transparent in letting you all know that I've never had sex at the wine bar. Other local watering holes would get Mary Sue in a kinky mood for some reason and so I can't say the same for most restrooms around the Malibu area.

I never did see Bert drink. I speculated it was because he didn't want to crash his walker but no, he'd make a point to say it was because of his beliefs in the CSCS. Members of the CSCS were forbidden to drink.

While Bert's legs didn't work so good other things sure did. As old as he was, his head could and would move with lightning speed when he'd see a good-looking young lady walk by. I think that was because Bert was always on the lookout for new clients. I don't think he saw people as air breathers ever. What he saw was the snip snip here and the snip snip there in everybody. As he saw it, he stood up for an opportunity for true equality. He did his part to try and make each and every one of us look the same.

CHAPTER 5

A Brief Introduction to Sloths

One day I got an unusual phone call. The call had come from Mary Sue, and she wanted me to meet her at the house. The house was actually his house but because she hated the thought of it not being hers one day, she always referred to Bert's house as "the" house. Anyhow, it wasn't very far away. It wouldn't take me long to get there - and so I went.

Driving through Malibu I wondered what it would be like to live in such a place. I think anyone who had any ambition would find it hard not to. When I got there, a young lady who looked like Mary Sue came barging out of the two massive front doors and into the driveway. I make mention that she looked like Mary Sue because she sure didn't act like Mary Sue. Mary Sue was a sweet Midwest... "That mother fucker... that mother fucker... that mother fucker," Mary Sue said while throwing garbage bags into the back of my van. "He finally did it. He gave every last penny to the goddamn Church of Science & Celebrities & Stuff. They are going to take the fucking house, brother."

Ever had a woman you've been having sex with call you brother? It's weird, right? I looked at all the garbage bags now in my van. "Is this all your stuff?" I asked. I wasn't trying to be a smartass. It was an honest question, but Mary Sue didn't say nothing. So, I decided to dish out my never-fail non sequitur to chill out the mood.

"Ever wonder how sloths have sex, Mary Sue?"

A tough cookie. She didn't even crack a smile at my question. I continued on anyhow. "So, it's actually kind of interesting. It's the only thing they do quickly. Sloth sex only lasts one minute and then they are done. It's a true bing, bong, boom and then they go back to being slothy."

Not flinching, she looked on at me emotionless. I decided to continue on. "Yeah, the males even hang out close to the females so they can keep going at it for a few days. Sloth males, and actually sloth females too, will have sex with any other sloth as well. I mean sloths get down wild, man," I told her. Mary Sue continued staring at me. I looked back at all the garbage bags. "Does this mean you are moving in with me by the way?"

"No, I wouldn't move in with you. I'd move back to Missouri before moving in with you, Jesus. Now come help me grab more shit," she said.

"We aren't stealing this old guy's stuff, are we?" I asked her. "No, and don't ask stupid shit," she replied. I was pretty certain we were totally stealing the old guy's stuff after that.

"Want to know anything else about sloths?" I asked.

CHAPTER 6

A Shag Palace

Mary Sue had never acted like this before. I immediately questioned if what I was witnessing was her true self now before me. Maybe she was a better actress than I had realized. She was usually very sweet and never swore. She always played the part to make the most out of any situation. After all, she had moved out here to get ahead. Not to fall behind. While she had come across to me as very calculating, what I was seeing before me was brazen anger. Pure uncalculated fueled craziness. I looked inside my glovebox for a Xanax to give her, but I didn't have any. I was a problem-finder but not always a solution-maker.

The inside of Bert's house was massive. I'd be hard-pressed to even call it a home. It had been built in the 1920s for someone who must have liked harems and art deco terrazzo floors. As an FYI terrazzo floors look like linoleum with little rocks in them. Think high school hallway. To me, they've always looked like prettied-up concrete. Anyhow, regardless of how good or bad you think terrazzo floors look, hard floors in a sex palace wouldn't make for the best combination if you think about it. I wondered who had made this executive decision. So now that we all have a visual on the floors, let's delve into the rest of Bert's place.

The walls... the walls were covered with finely detailed tapestries of regal gardens. While a nice thought, the patrons of the gardens were half-goat people indulging in wild orgies. I'm not sure if I've ever heard of a boring orgy but just in case - people always make a point to put the word "wild" in front of the word orgy and so to stay true to any readers that are swingers the scenes were quite the "wild" orgy event. My lesson learned here was that if you are half human and half goat there must be a rule that you are only allowed to have sexy time in a garden. Was it because of the smell? I made a mental note. It's important to make mental notes. You never know what the future beholds.

On to the statuary... Every statue, and there were aplenty, were of all sorts of animals making love. I am a fan of both National Geographic and the Discovery Channel, so I have seen many an animal bang in my time, but I'd never seen any animal sex look as pleasant as it did here amongst this fine statuary.

To me, sex in the animal kingdom had always looked rapey as hell. So, it was nice to see the compliment of happy animal sex statues in what I could only describe as a tribute to all of the animal kingdom enjoying first base more than hitting a home run. With all that being said I couldn't help but note that the elephant dong seemed to be larger than the sperm whale dong. I wondered if that was the artistic license of the sculptor or in fact quite calculated. I made a second mental note to remember the fine artist who had signed each and every piece with their initials 'AP.' Maybe, I'd find this 'AP' someday and have the chance to ask about the dongs of each statue.

The only thing missing in the rooms were hanging pieces of loose fabric. All harems to me had buttresses of fabric hanging on all the ceilings. I don't know why it was important to hide harem ceilings but maybe the fabric was put there to keep the smell of sex within the rooms. The opposite of the goat people sex parties which were apparently held outdoors. Another reason could have been the one I had had in my house years earlier.

I had hung fabric in my house once because the popcorn ceilings had begun to fall down, and I didn't want to hear about asbestos poisoning from any bleeding-heart liberals that came to visit. I was proud of my quick fix back then and only now had I figured the only reason ancient harems hadn't done the same thing as I was because they hadn't yet invented popcorn.

The last value-added accompaniment in the main house were the gold tassels. There's nothing really to say about those, but they really did compliment the space. I don't know what it is about dangly bits, but I sure do love them.

"Hey, Mary Sue, do you mind if I use the restroom? I have to shock the monkey," I asked. "Why can't men just ask where the bathroom is? I don't care what you need to do in there, brother. You can just ask," she replied. I looked at her blankly. "The monkey... I" Mary Sue interrupted me. "You go down that hallway and the third door on your right will lead you through another hallway. When you get to the end of that, make a left and the bathroom is right there. It's really not that hard to find," she explained.

Now, I didn't really have to take a leak. It just seems like a more polite thing to say than "Hey, can I take a shit in your house." Well, Bert's house or whoever's it was. I followed her directions and when I got to the restroom, I sat down on the solid gold toilet with a pearl inlay handle and pondered all. What was the meaning of all this? Why so much terrazzo? My guess was the floors had at one point been covered in throw rugs. That would certainly be my orgy fix? If I had mistakenly put in hard floors. It would be super expensive but whoever built this place clearly didn't care about money. People who don't care about money often do strange things. My next question to pontificate upon while doing my business was why were the walls padded in this room?

And then... When I looked up to wipe my ass, I saw them. Fabric buttresses covering the ceilings. There in laid my answer. They were in fact to keep the smell in. I was excited I figured out at least something today.

"Hey, shithead, you going to help or what?" Mary Sue yelled from outside the door breaking my train of thought. "You know it is literally called the restroom!" I yelled back through the door. I hurried up and washed my hands as it had now been made clear there was some sort of great urgency to the situation.

CHAPTER 7

Boogie Woogie

Mary Sue threw open two floor-to-ceiling doors to reveal a great library. It would print well to say the library was endless, but it was in fact only two mid-sized rooms. Which still, of course, made for a very sizable library. The walls of both rooms were formed from carved mahogany. The place in short smelled like smart people.

"All these books. Everyone in the room. I want every shelf emptied," she told me. We were of course standing in the second room. The room farther from the van. "What about that room?" I asked. I pointed towards the first room that had less books in it. "No, leave that room alone. I like that room," she replied. Mary Sue handed me a pile of books. "Go, shoo," she said.

Looking at the pile of books I saw they all had the same title. "These are all the same book. Who has a library of the same book?" I asked. "He bought eight copies of everything. One for each one of his snot-nosed grandkids. There are cases of DVD's next door. We are going to trash all those too," she told me.

"Any of his grandkids blind?" I asked her.

"No, why? That's an odd thing to ask," Mary Sue replied.

"Just wondering, I always figured the worst part about being blind would be if you had to let a snot rocket go and then couldn't find the booger on your shirt. You know, because you're blind."

"No, I never thought about that," Mary Sue replied. My non-sequiturs were suckin'.

"What is all this shit?" I asked, changing the conversation topic once again. Most of the books in the room were still factory shrink-wrapped. "The Church of Science & Celebrities & Stuff, bro. The CSCS," she replied. Not really understanding how I got wrapped up in this, I emptied the room into my van like a good little helper and didn't ask any more questions.

My van completely full, fenders kissing the Malibu dirt, she sent me on my way. I'd like to say that was the end of it, but it wasn't. I had to do three separate trips packed to the rafters with just CSCS books and DVD's.

My instructions were to take them all to the dump. So, I did, I dumped them right smack dab in the middle of my living room. My living room was now a written-down collective of what I imagined went through Tom Cruise's brain daily. My little air shrine now was a maze of floor-to-ceiling Church of Science & Celebrities & Stuff stuff. My plan – sell it all on eBay.

CHAPTER 8

The American Dream – Two Generations of Commitment

People question the meaning of life. I didn't have time for that, what I did question, repeatedly, was why I had to empty a room of heavy books.

The real answer was simple. There was of course an explanation. What Mary Sue had told me through overexaggerated hysteria was that Bert had given so much money to the CSCS that his house was now in foreclosure. What that meant was Mary Sue's worst fear was coming true. She was going to get nothing. She'd go back to Missouri like her mother had done before her with nothing as well. Two generations of failure.

All the time she had spent in Hollywood had been a waste. I didn't understand what getting rid of all his CSCS books solved but the wrath of a woman who feels scorned is unmerciful. There is nothing like hitting a man in the jugular like taking away his bible books. While that was her answer, my reasoning was much more simple. I was moving heavy books because the girl I was sleeping with told me to.

CHAPTER 9

Speak, Tommy Baby!

After bearing witness to the wrath of Mary Sue I decided to take a break from hanging out with her. I had said earlier I had become bored of watching American-made porn and that was true. But now, not seeing Mary Sue it didn't take long for me to not be sick of it at all. Focus changes all the time, and I had begun to focus on watching American-made porn while skimming through the endless supply of the word of the CSCS's doctrine, maybe better known as Tom Cruise speak.

BOOK 2

THE PAST

CHAPTER 10

We live in the present, most certainly don't talk about the future enough, and rarely put much time into thinking about our past. Maybe it's because we can't change any of the above. Or maybe it is because we are programmed to drift along. It's all up to you. You can drift along like a floating turd down a sewer waterway, or you could strive to be that same turd turding your way along on a bitchin' water park slide. The choice is yours, my friend!

I'm going to tell you about my past a little. I'm doing that because it's very cool when an author makes everything come full circle. That is what writers do to get the "aha" moments readers all cherish. You will "aha" here shortly.

Tracing back through the annals of Steve history. I had wasted all my money on making a movie. The idea of becoming a director seemed like a fun one and so in that pursuit, I had put all my money into a low-budget feature film. Contrary to what I know were your first thoughts. It was not a porn film but a real genuine art film. If you ever want to see your money evaporate, I urge you to try making an art film as well. I probably should have made a porn movie.

Totally broke, I moved in with a friend into a large five-bedroom house and together we started growing weed. At first, we sucked at it. I was pulling weeds out of my sidewalk, but couldn't grow marijuana out of perfectly organic PH-tested soil. The truth is it could have also been that instead of focusing on our grow, we were throwing parties every weekend and having mini-parties every day. Either way, between the weed and the partying life was exciting.

Our friend, Pete Peterson, yes that is his real name, had been born into porn. He started a blog with the same name and the stories he posted there were about his odd upbringing. Pete's blog had shifted my reading time focus, and I no longer read National Geographic. His postings were always hilarious.

His background was that his dad worked as an adult film model agent. Just like mainstream actresses' adult actresses had begun to get signed up with agents as well. Pete's job was to get all the personal information from the new "talent" and take photos of them nude to start shopping around to the industry. It wasn't all about Pete's dad. His mom was cool too. She worked at the crepe stand outside the local BBQ restaurant. She was a crepe master. She knew just the right amount of strawberry preservative to rub on my crepe every time. I think it would be a gross way of underpraising her to call her just a crepe genius. If all the crepe-making ladies on the planet were Greek Goddesses Pete's mom would hands down be Athena.

Because of who Pete's father was, hopefully you're done envisioning Pete's mom now, Pete was a direct conduit to women with questionable standards. As new "drug" dealers Tim and I felt right at home consorting with these young ladies doing their best to enrich the lives of men across the world. I began selling all the ladies that would come and go from Pete's place California grown Marijuana. I was finally turning into the man my mom could be proud of. I was making my own money and rubbing shoulders with many a shoe model actress from mostly Florida. In summation, here I was creating my own lasting memories.

The house rules were simple. If you had done any porn shoots that day you had to jump in the spa before rubbing up on anything in the house. Second rule - if Pete is hanging out you can't stand in front of the TV and talk. Naked or not. It didn't matter. Those were the rules.

Pete fascinated me. A straight male, he had still become so accustomed to female nudity that he genuinely preferred to play video games over looking at naked women. I envied him for it. It was like a superpower to me. In turn, it also amazed me that though the young ladies were aware of the house rules they still always stood in front of the TV trying to talk to Pete. This would infuriate him, and thus it became a house rule. Tim and I loved boobies, girls making out, tongues, tits, feet, orifices, fingers, round parts, pointy parts, voluptuous parts, lippy parts, nosy parts, long hair, short hair - did I mention boobs? I forget. Anyhow, all sorts of other female anatomy. In front of the TV though, that was unacceptable! Why? Because... well, because Pete was our friend.

If you are envisioning a sex-crazed constant orgy house, I appreciate that, but no - that was not really the case. The women though usually naked, mostly because of the house spa requirement, never really had sex in the house. They were tired from having sex all day and their lady parts were also understandably tired as well. So, instead, we'd all play the Nintendo game *Mario Kart*.

CHAPTER 11

A "Safe" Space

It wasn't all about women. Remember, this was supposed to be a marijuana segue. I hope you are still waiting for the "aha" moment.

Initially, Tim and I grew weed in the master closet of the house. We had made a big sliding mirrored door, hiding the doorway, and with it on, it didn't look like there was a closet there at all. The door opened with a magnetic lock. The only way to open the door was by de-magnetizing the lock. To do so we had a key that you'd have to insert into a dummy outlet. We were very proud of ourselves. It was honestly super slick. It was cool for real.

Inside we had gutted the master closet and put all the nice shelving that had been in there in the garage. In that closet, we fit four grow lights. We covered those lights with tinfoil so that police helicopters couldn't pick up on the house having a grow room with their high-end heat sensor technology. That was Tim's idea! We were truly a state-of-the-art operation. We were off to making millions. To start making millions our goal was to harvest one pound per light. In those days a pound of good weed sold for forty-eight hundred dollars. So, if we didn't screw up - the room would yield nineteen thousand dollars every few months.

A month or so into our first grow, the room got too hot and it burned up all the plants. I blamed the tin foil hats on the grow lights. Whatever had done it, we were screwed. We clipped up what we had, and totaled up, it came to a quarter pound of burned-up crap. I had been the one who had come up with the money to pay the rent and so this hurt.

Our second round didn't do well either. We got spider mites. Spider mites make a web around the weed and eat it from the inside out. They reminded me of the person who picks all the good stuff out of Rocky Road ice cream and then leaves the rest of the ice cream in the paper carton. Savages!

Weed was rough. I was getting my clock cleaned. It was time to properly learn how to do this. It was time for less *Mario Kart* and more weed.

CHAPTER 12

Bring a Friend

Around this time, I ran back into my friend Atsushi. Sometimes, the universe smiles down upon us. In Atsushi's case, the smile came more like a dumb grin with constant cottonmouth behind chompers and red eyes - not staring into your soul but staring into nothing. Atsushi hailed from Northern California. Nor Cal is also known as the home of all things marijuana. Not to generalize too much but those hippies up there sure do like weed.

Atsushi looked like a mix between Keanu Reeves and Fabio. His sole interest in life was to sleep with women. Not one, but always two at a time. You know that song "One" by Harry Nilsson. Three Dog Night sang it too. "One is the loneliest number that you'll ever do." That's the first line of the song if you don't know it, and that is the farthest Atsushi had made it into the track. However, he took that line to heart.

I don't know what clicked in his brain to think the song was really about threesomes but what the hell do I know about music? Maybe there was a sale on patchouli oil that he was reading about while listening to the track, and that got him horny. Either way, with Atsushi's newfound wisdom, he decided that threesomes were the only thing worth living for. I didn't understand it. If I was in a threesome and another dude was involved, I'd just be focused on trying to get to the hole before the other guy made it there.

I hadn't seen Atsushi in years. Pre-threesome life, we had been friends when he was in college down in San Diego. No, wait a minute. Sorry, it's been a long time. I was in college, his roommates were in college, his girlfriend was in college, and Atsushi… well he just spent a lot of time at college bars.

When not spending his time learning at college bars, he spent the rest of his time working at sushi bars. That's right - I said sushi bars and not sushi bar. You see, Atsushi had been rightfully fired from literally every single decent sushi spot in San Diego and its surrounding areas.

I know this is all a bit confusing. When I first met Atsushi, it confused me too. "So, your name is Atsushi?" I asked. "No man. It's not at sushi, it's Atsushi," he replied. "And you work at sushi places, dude?" I asked. "That's right, Columbo," he replied. "Yeah, that's really confusing, man," I said. Atsushi had heard this before. "Maybe you should work at an Italian restaurant instead?" I got nothing from Atsushi. "Or don't you have a middle name you can use?" I suggested. "My middle name is Aoi," he replied. "Oh man, that's a rough one. Seriously? That a real name or did your mom make these all up?" Atsushi did not respond. "Atsushi Aoi Smith," I said his full name aloud. Atsushi stared straight ahead, not saying a word. "Got it. Cool. Go, mom, man!" I said. That was the end of the conversation.

The final frontier, literally the last sushi joint within a hundred-mile radius, was one of those revolving sushi spots. In those places, the sushi spins around the bar on a conveyor belt, and you grab what you want to eat. When you are done eating, they count the plates and then the restaurant charges you per empty plate. If the sushi isn't too bad you get food poisoning while at home and not while you are still in the restaurant.

I had gone to meet him at his revolving sushi restaurant. The plan was I'd hang around in the restaurant doing my own thing, until he got off of work. His shift being almost over, it wouldn't be that big of a deal. Once Atsushi clocked out, then we could go learn about some beer at a local college dive bar. I sat down at the revolving sushi bar and leaned forward to grab one of the plates. It had been a two-and-a-half-hour drive from Los Angeles to San Diego and I figured I'd eat a little bit before going out and getting hammered with Atsushi. I picked a plate that looked like a California roll for obvious reasons. Before I could eat it, Atsushi put up his hand and stopped me. "You don't want to eat that shit man." I put the plate back on the conveyor belt. "It will be fine dude. It's not fish," I said, not thinking that I was telling a guy who makes sushi for a living what's in a California roll.

A Japanese man, presumably the owner of the sushi conveyor belt bar, looked over to see what was going on. I smiled at him with a huge grin in an effort to let him know that I wasn't complaining about his fine eating establishment.

However, what was going on was Atsushi was about to make me full on Atsushi style sushi instead of making the rolls he was supposed to be making.

Now, the reason Atsushi kept getting hired at sushi restaurants was because he was a no-joke sushi chef, but I assure you this place wasn't where top chefs worked. To make a living at these places, you had to keep the people coming in and out as fast as the plates moving around on the conveyor belts did. Atsushi stopping to make me "real rolls" would slow down the plates and crush this guy's pocketbook.

A big argument ensued in Japanese between Atsushi and his boss. I watched on with a couple other people as we heard a lot of angry Japanese talk with the words "mother fucker" mixed in all over the place. I don't know what the other people were thinking, but I was wondering if mother fucker was in or out of context. What if it was the only word he knew in English and he was switching out mother fucker with the word, please? "You make that sushi you worthless human being, mother fucker/please." I wasn't sure what was going on, but more and more I was thinking that there were no pleases being thrown around in the mix.

Instead of sorting it out or doing what he was told, Atsushi unabashedly put his headset on in front of his boss and kept making me sushi. The boss guy got angrier and angrier. I tried talking to Atsushi, but he blew me off too. Plate after plate of awesome sushi kept appearing in front of me. "Here is your Uramaki, sir. Here is your Yukiwa-maki, sir." After a few minutes, he was handing me more plates than any one person would ever be able to eat. I didn't know what he was talking about but every time he said Uramaki or Yukiwa-maki he'd smile over at the boss who was now throwing rice and shit all over the kitchen.

When Atsushi and I left to grab beers not too much later two things had happened, I was now extremely full, and Atsushi once again was unemployed. When his girlfriend found out we both knew she'd go berserk. I didn't know if she was into twosomes or threesomes but either way, Atsushi wasn't going to be included in either for a while.

For the next two days, we hid from the girlfriend and drank like rich college students. After forty-eight hours of continuous partying, the last thing I remember was listening to Atsushi get torn apart by his lady while I was passed out on the couch. It was moments like these I was glad I didn't have a girlfriend.

When I woke up the next day Atsushi was gone. His girlfriend and he had gotten into such a big FU Match that he had left. That night he got so drunk, he stole a bicycle - I assume to drive home. It wouldn't have been cool to do under any conditions but Atsushi's situation was bad. The bicycle was actually a police bike. Even lamer, Atsushi had stolen it while the cop was standing next to the bike. The cop was only a few feet away giving someone a drunk in public ticket. Atsushi hadn't even made it a block on his new cop cruiser before he got beaten down by a flock of police officers. I always thought a group of policemen should have a name. Like a flock or a herd or a troop. So, I'm calling them a flock, because these cops flew in and beat the ever-living shit out of my poor thieving piece of shit friend Atsushi. Needless to say, he didn't make it home on the bike that night.

CHAPTER 13

Slow Down, Mr. Turtle

After San Diego Atsushi had moved back home to Santa Clara, California. I learned he was traveling back and forth from Northern California to Los Angeles a few times a week for business. I'm sure it is obvious to you what his business now was but at the time I was clueless. I sure as hell knew it wasn't selling beach cruisers, but I figured he was coming down to Los Angeles to meet women and cater sushi events.

It took a few trips, but when Atsushi and I did manage to meet up with one another we did so at a place in Los Angeles called Brennans. Brennen's had been there forever. Their thing, or their gimmick, is they have turtle racing on the patio every Thursday night. What goes down is everyone stands around in a circle and all watch turtle's race. If anyone is caught pointing at any of the turtles in the race, the event stops, and the person has to "donate" money to the people who promote the event. It's fun until it gets irritating because more often than not someone points at the fucking turtle, and they stop the race. The gimmick is lame because it happens EVERY race and the turtles never actually finish. It becomes an annoying money grab.

While hanging out inside at Brennan's, Atsushi and I got to talking. Though the turtle racing was outside, I had brought my drunk pal Jackson, and he kept pointing at all the turtles in kind of a swoop-like fashion. He was either too drunk to point, or he was afraid there was a field sobriety test mixed in with this turtle stuff somehow. With his masterful lightsaber swoop-type point, he was stopping the race each time and then throwing change at the turtle racing handler guys. I knew he was going to get kicked out soon, so Atsushi and I had gone inside. When he got tossed into the street, we'd pretend we didn't know him.

Jackson, though a total drunk, was an interesting cat. Jackson had started a teddy bear company while still in high school. While Atsushi and I, and probably you, were smoking weed and drinking booze he had been smart.

Jackson had reached out to Longs Drugs when he was something like fifteen years old and got the buyer's information who bought for the gift aisle in the store. It turned out the buyer was an old lady. He set up an appointment and brought her a basket of teddy bears to check out. She, thinking it was all cute as hell, ended up buying stuffed animals from him for every Longs Drugs location - five hundred and twenty-one to be exact. From there he expanded to sell stuffed animals to every presidential library in the nation all while still in high school. A few years later he had sold the company for millions.

Anyhow, Atsushi and I watched on as my dumbass drunk pal Jackson got chucked into the street. He actually didn't get kicked out for tossing change at anyone though. He got booted because he had got up on the stage and was trying to fight the singer of the cover band. Jackson, a huge Henry Rollins fan, was yelling at the guy in more broken English than Atsushi's old sushi boss. What he had been trying to tell the guy was that he had no right being on the stage singing because he wasn't Henry Rollins. It sounded more like, "No Rollins! No Rollins... You suck." I knew what he meant, but no one else seemed to. Jackson could have gone into chemistry. Not Henry Rollins = No Sing. The equation was simple. Once in the middle of the street he almost got hit by a few cars before security came to find me so that he didn't get run over.

What's important about all of this was that before leaving I had told Atsushi that I had been growing weed with Tim, but we were not doing so well. Nodding, Atsushi had told me, "I'll help you out." It was some Keanu Reeves/ Fabio Godfather-type shit, and I couldn't wait to tell Tim. I didn't know if he could help us out or not, but I soon found out he sure could.

CHAPTER 14

A Mario Toad

Next time he drove down for "business," Atsushi stayed at Tim and I's place. Walking through the front door, he brought duffle bag after duffle bag into our house. I didn't know if they were all filled with weed, or if he was moving into the place. He opened two of the duffle bags and that put any questions we had to rest. Each bag was filled with vacuum-sealed pounds of the prettiest marijuana I'd ever seen.

Tim loved it all, but it made me nervous. I had never seen that much weed. The most I had ever seen handled in one place was probably five pounds. Atsushi had brought hundreds. This dirt foot Nor Cal hippy was going to get us in a lot of trouble.

Yet, one thing outweighed any fear and that was the lack of money in my pocketbook. Atsushi would be the one to save us. Tim and I didn't really have a plan B. I mean if this didn't work out, we didn't know what we could do. Neither one of us had any sort of a resume. I wouldn't have hired me.

I never got used to selling weed, but I knew that day buying and selling smoke was going to be my future for a while. I buttered up to Atsushi and told him when in town he could save on hotel costs and start staying with Tim and me all the time if he liked. He jumped at the opportunity. I'm sure all the porn chicks helped persuade him just a little bit as well.

While telling Atsushi the house rules Tim proudly showed him our little grow operation. Instead of giving us accolades, he laughed. As he laughed a little puff of stoner fuel popped up from his chest and out through his mouth.

All very matter of fact, Tim and I closed the mirrored grow room door. As we all walked back downstairs to sit on the couch, Atsushi instead walked right out the front door. Tim and I sat there wondering why he left. Actually, that's not true. We didn't. We started playing *Mario Kart* again. When Atsushi got back from his car, he threw a copy of *High Times Magazine* on the table but neither one of us reached for it.

"I got you, bitch. Yoshi is going to take you out!" Tim yelled in my face. I played Toad. I wasn't worried. Toad was the best character hands down. I was going to win, and I knew it. Atsushi stood up, grabbed the magazine back, threw the magazine directly in my face, and then went into the kitchen. Sure enough, on the front cover of the magazine was our grow system. The tubes, the volcanic rock, everything. Atsushi walked back into the room with a lit-up mighty joint. I'd quickly learn this was a regular occurrence. He smoked weed all day.

"There is nothing new about growing hydroponically man," he said. I stopped playing the game and Tim focused on beating me. "Read up and learn how to do it right," he said.

"Look in all seriousness. You can help me sell this stuff, right?" I said to him. Atsushi didn't answer. We both knew he could, and he would. We were friends.

Taking a minute to register everything, I was now mad. I had been acting like an asshole. I'd prefer to be a Mario Toad. A winner, every time. Atsushi smiled from ear to ear. He was stoned and happy with his side of the deal too. Tim... well Tim was just happy to beat me in the game.

All decided, Tim turned on *Scrubs*, his favorite TV show on the planet, while Atsushi and I headed out to the backyard to figure some of this stuff out.

CHAPTER 15

No More Partying in the Closet

Everything happened fast. We tore our kickass top-secret closet grow room apart and put all the shelving back into it. Then we took one of the spare bedrooms and blew it up. Blow it up means to build a grow room. Our grow room was now three times the size it had been before. With Atsushi in the mix, I knew I could sell more weed. I just needed to have more weed to sell.

Soon, the parties at the house got bigger. We were excited about everything and started having ragers. We had to put deadbolt locks on every door in the house so that no one found our grow or wandered into the bedrooms. It was cool, it was all working out, and most importantly because of Atsushi, we were finally going to be making money!

CHAPTER 16

What Happens in Vegas Stays in Vegas

To make a few much-needed dollars in the interim, I drove a pound of lemon OG to Las Vegas and sold it for six thousand dollars. Driving to Vegas meant crossing over a state line. That meant if I got busted it would be a federal crime and not a state crime. That was bad. On the upside federal prisons are nicer than state ones.

Now who would pay six thousand dollars for a pound of weed? Even if someone was crossing state lines to get it to you. Even if it was the best Cali weed money can buy. Who? Who would do that crazy? Noah Higgins that's who.

I had met Noah in a bar in Beverly Hills years earlier. I was there hanging out with this wanna-be producer guy. The guy told everyone always that he was friends with Justin Timberlake. I was continuously amazed at how many conversations a committed person could have and slyly slide Justin Timberlake's name into it.

"Hey man, you hungry? Wanna grab some lunch?" I'd ask. "Nah, man. I just had lunch with Justin Timberlake. Man does that guy like eggs," he'd say. "That's cool," I'd reply.

"Hey man, wanna go to a Superbowl party?" I'd ask. "Na, going to Justin Timberlake's. I'm bringing deviled eggs," he'd say. "That's cool," I'd reply.

"Yo, brother wanna go to the Swedish Bikini Team All Nude Spa Festival" I'd ask. "How are they a Swedish Bikini Team if they are all nude?" he'd reply. That one made sense. I didn't really have an answer for that.

However, he continued on, and I was waiting for it, "... I can't go anyhow though. I'm going to a chicken farm with Justin Timberlake to give eggs away to inner city children." "Oh, OK. That's cool" I'd then reply.

Wouldn't you call a guy you hung out with that much by his first name only? I never asked him that. I didn't want to embarrass the guy.

Eventually, it actually worked. Someone did let him produce something. Keep shaking that tree I tell ya! That someone wasn't really a someone but more of a something. The Kabala Center hired him to produce some documentary. The doc was cool. It had Madonna in it, Roseanne, and if I remember correctly Monica Lewinsky. No Justin Timberlake though. He definitely should have included his good pal.

So, what did the producer really do for a living? He was a trust fund kid whose parents paid his bills. For extra money he sold cocaine. And that my friends is the real Hollywood in a nutshell.

I met Noah while hanging out with that dude. Noah owned some life raft company out of Australia. He got me selling the exclusive rights to sell his life rafts in different regions of the United States. I did pretty well on it too.

Noah's love of Australia wasn't mutual. He had been kicked out of Australia for fraud, and his life raft company was in major legal turmoil. He was a crooked Canuck. They had sent him back to Canada, and at some point, he had made his way down to Los Angeles. I wasn't sure if Noah was proud to have been born in Canada. I was proud to have been born in Los Angeles and I wondered all the time if a cheetah was glad to have been born in Africa. Maybe one day we would all switch places and see how the rest of our lives went. I knew the cheetah would do fine in Los Angeles. There are lots of people who have cheetah skin purses and jackets here. But before I make any deals, I'd need to know if they have any good beer in Africa.

The life raft company was a nightmare for me. Noah had sold the exclusive rights to life rafts that didn't exist. There were none. I worked my butt off to pay all those people back. I paid everyone back but one guy who thought the situation was so funny that he didn't really care about the money.

So, why did I still play in the sandbox with the guy? Maybe it was because he gave me six thousand dollars for weed when I was selling it for forty-eight hundred.

CHAPTER 17

Swimming in Horse Money

Noah had picked a bunch of the horses correctly in the Kentucky Derby and now had some money in his pocket. I knew he wouldn't have it for long, so I rushed out to Vegas to see him weed in hand.

Noah had been sleeping on some random dude's couch. This dude was almost forty years old and lived with his parents. How Noah worked his way into living on the guy's parents' couch was unknown to me. When Noah was a kid back in the nineteen seventies he had sold encyclopedias door to door in Canada. That's gotta be tough! He was a born salesman, but he was greedy. No deal was ever to make a couple grand. Every deal was to make a few million bucks. None of those deals worked out - and so he lived on some guy's couch with that guy's family.

I hid the money Noah gave me for the weed under the back seat of my car, and the two of us accompanied by Noah's adopted family hit the town.

Noah loved strip clubs. On the way to the strip club, we stopped off at a casino because he needed to place a quick bet. Historically I had loaned money to Noah to bet with. When he won, he'd pay me off big. When he lost, I'd figure out other ways to get my money back.

As an example, since Noah was a gambling addict he was owed a lot of money in taxes. I had made a deal with him that if I paid his accountant fees, and loaned him some money on top of it, I would get all his tax return money. It of course didn't go as planned. He got randomly audited. It took me forever to get that money, but I did eventually get it, and I made a good profit.

On this trip Noah didn't need my money. He was swimming in cash. He had won over forty grand on the Kentucky Derby. I tried to get him to give me some money to put aside for him so that he could find himself an apartment, but he was sure Floyd Mayweather Jr. would lose his next fight. He kept ten grand to blow on partying that night and bet the rest of it on the Mayweather fight. On the way out of the hotel where he made the bet we ran into Phil.

I had met Phil a year or so earlier. My sister had been invited to the Australian Consul General's house on a date. I can't remember why, but my mom and I ended up tagging along. The event was accompanied by an Aboriginal art show. I really don't care for Aboriginal art and so I found myself drinking beer after beer with some fella who seemed to know everyone at the place. That fella was Phil. I found out later he wasn't just any ol' popular guy at the party either. He WAS the consul general. Phil and I started hanging out all the time. His wife didn't like going to movie screenings and I was all about going anywhere that I could drink for free. Part of his job was to be seen out and about at Australian events and so we'd hit up movies that were made by Aussies or had Australian film stars in them. It was great. We got along well and always had a lot of fun.

To be candid, my relationship with Phil was a slow brew. When guys give each other their personal information it doesn't mean they are ever going to hang out. Most of the time it means we will never see one another again. So, while Phil and I had exchanged information at the consul general's house, I added him to my party invite list and then completely forgot the guy existed.

The reason we started hanging out came months later. He had come to one of the parties at my house by accident. The party happened to be my birthday. Every year I throw a chili cookoff and they kickass. He thought he was going to some other guy's kickass birthday. As soon as Phil arrived, he found out that when it came to partying, Tim and I were pros. We might have sucked at growing weed but we sure knew how to throw a party. Phil had brought VB (Victoria Bitters), which is a beer you can't get in the States. Of course, a popular guy at the party amongst all my Australian friends. By the end of the party, Phil was family. We were inseparable after that.

CHAPTER 18

Merriweather VS Noah

So, Noah, the guy whose parents owned the couch Noah lived on, and I cruised out of the hotel. The first person we saw outside the casino door randomly was my friend Phil. He had just gotten out of his limo with whom I would later find out was his son. I literally put my hand on his shoulder and turned his consul general ass back around to climb back into the limo. I didn't even say hi to him. It was a streamlined performance. It was like we had set it up, but we hadn't.

Looking around the limo, from face to face, this group was an odd one. There was no doubt about it. All together, in a limo drinking the cheap soda pops that always come in a limo, we drove to some high-end strip club off the Las Vegas strip.

The first round was three thousand dollars. Noah ordered bottles of Dom Perignon to celebrate. Part of Noah's end game here was to buddy up with Phil. As mentioned, Noah had been banned from going back into Australia because of the life raft scheme. He wanted to go live there again one day and thought Phil was the guy who could make something like that happen.

The night flurried by. Noah kept burning fifty-dollar bills to show the strippers he didn't care about money, and I kept blowing the flame out and putting the burned bills in my pockets. After the ten thousand dollars he had reserved for the night was spent, we all crashed out in some killer suites at the Hard Rock Hotel courtesy of you guessed it - Noah Higgins.

If you are a boxing fan you know. Floyd Merriweather didn't lose the fight. And so, Noah lived on that guy's couch for another year or so. The dude's dad ended up dying, and Noah got kicked out by the fella's mom. The saddest part about the story was Noah was still never allowed back to Australia. So much for my nice feel-good happy ending.

Driving back home I felt rich! I hadn't had any money in my pocket in a while. And now I had a whole bunch. To celebrate I took out a couple girlfriends. It was a night of drunken debauchery and a ton of fun. On the way home... I got a DUI. If you are sober enough to remember your DUI it is a total buzz kill. Life is full of ups and downs. The six thousand dollars I had made from Noah disappeared as fast as his Kentucky Derby money did, but for five minutes I had felt like a king.

Something had to give. Things were tough. I was getting ahead, but it was a slow process. I couldn't go back to Vegas to sell anymore weed either. Noah had no more money. I sat at home and idly watched my weed grow.

CHAPTER 19

Bomb.com

When Atsushi came back through, I had taken over the full duties of growing the weed. My first round was good. I knew it, and I was proud of it. I showed Atsushi the strain called Jack Herer that we had been growing. Atsushi looked at the Jack, smelled it, and then closely inspected it. A true connoisseur, he was taking this job very seriously. Tim and I stared at him eyes wide. We were like kids in a candy shop with a surprise visit from Willy Wonka.

Tim broke the silence blurting out, "Fuckin' bomb, huh?" Atsushi didn't acknowledge the remark. He stood resolute, inspecting the prized nugget. I knew it was really good, mostly because Tim kept saying so. But now we had to get rid of it and make money. I needed to change our green in for (in the words of Ray Charles) some "Greenback Dollar Bills."

We didn't have much more time to make this thing really work and I knew it. I couldn't afford all the expenses. It wasn't just rent. It was all the nutrients, the lights, paying the clippers, buying the grow cubes. All of it. It was all expensive stuff. Atsushi was the connection to making it all happen, or we were gonna fail. That was the long and short of it.

CHAPTER 20

I REALLY Gotta Go

It wasn't all one-sided though. While in town this time, Atsushi needed my help. If not my help, he was going to need someone's help. He had broken his leg and was scrambling around on crutches. Jumping on an electric skateboard he'd run smack dab into a wall. Fucken' stoners.

Hanging out with him meant maybe I could help facilitate getting rid of the three pounds of Jack Herer Tim and I had to sell. Together we loaded the duffle bags into the back of his Suburban.

Now, I'm dumb and so while I knew there was weed in the duffle bags, I figured the bags were mostly filled with Atsushi's clothes. This was a lot of weed. Maybe he was planning on staying with us for a while this time around?

To be honest though, maybe it was wishful thinking. Maybe I knew better, and maybe I just didn't want to confront what I was about to do... either way, I told myself that the bags were mostly clothes. I felt "cool" leaving with Atsushi, but I was also nervous as all hell. Atsushi and I left my house in West Hills, California, and headed down to Orange County, California in his nineteen-eighties Chevy Suburban. Whatever I had eaten for breakfast was really not sitting well and I was getting more and more eager to get to the destination. Driving down the 405 into Los Angeles proper, the Getty Museum on our right-hand side, I started to get the sweats. We still had an hour or so left on the freeway before we would get to Orange County and that was without traffic.

It was exciting to be hanging out with Atsushi. I was super stoked about possibly getting rid of some weed and even though all those things were running through my head. What was about to be running through my bottom was something not as exciting. You know when you gotta shit so bad you close your eyes and you kind of meditate? That's where I was. I was shit meditating when Atsushi pulled the Suburban to the side of the freeway. He lit up a joint and looked straight ahead. "Outta gas," he said. He didn't really say it to me. I wasn't sure who the hell he was talking to. The Suburban stunk of marijuana. There was no trunk for a cop to even open. You just had to look in the windows to see random huge duffel bags. And worse than all of this… I had to go to the bathroom something fierce. Atsushi and I sat on the side of the freeway and waited.

It didn't take too long, maybe three to five minutes, and a CHP car pulled up behind us. "It's a fucking cop," I concerningly said to Atsushi. Atsushi didn't seem to care at all. He just kept looking straight ahead. "Yep," was all he said. The genuine realization of going to jail hit me. What was worse was I was going to go to jail having shat myself.

The police officer walked down Atsushi's side of the Suburban. Nowadays, the highway patrol officer always walks up to the passenger window when I see cars on the side of the freeway getting pulled over. But back then they'd walk down to the driver's side window, traffic and all. I'll bet cops watched more John Wayne movies back then too.

Atsushi's window was already rolled down. Like Atsushi, the cop didn't seem to be too concerned either. "We all good here?" he said. Atsushi kind of flicked his head to the side and didn't say anything. "Outta gas or broke down?" he asked. Atsushi still didn't look at him. "Gas," was all he replied.

I figured if we got arrested, Atsushi would be the one in way more trouble than me. It wasn't my car, and I wasn't driving. I was just the guy next to him with the poop problem. In hindsight, I'm pretty sure I'm wrong. I think we would have both been in a lot of trouble.

The situation was in one word, "awkward." "Well, stay in the car, and roadside assistance will be here shortly," the police officer said. He didn't wait for a reply. He began to walk back to his patrol car. "I don't think I can take it, man. I seriously gotta go," I told Atsushi. Atsushi kind of chuckled. He didn't care about my "condition," and I think he realized we weren't going to be carted off to jail, at least not yet. Or maybe he was just so stoned he wasn't bothered either way.

The police officer sat in his car and in the distance, through the side mirror, I saw the roadside assistance truck pull to the shoulder of the freeway. As the police officer drove away the roadside assistance vehicle pulled into the spot where his patrol car had just been. I hopped out of the Suburban, but Atsushi didn't. Whether he wanted to or not I don't know; he was on crutches if you remember. I think in some twisted Atsushi way he was actually enjoying this situation. Atsushi had an odd deviant sense of humor.

I met the roadside assistance dude behind the Suburban. "Bro, can you give me a ride to the gas station? I gotta use the bathroom real bad," I said. "Truck broken or outta...," he started to ask. I interrupted him. "Outta gas," I said. I wanted to, no I needed to, hurry this situation along. "OK, I'll give you a gallon and you can drive to the gas station. There is one just up on the next offramp. You are literally right here." I nodded my head. "Alright, man," I replied. The guy gave us a little bit of gas and the Suburban started up. We rolled down the hill and got off at the next offramp. I thanked the Gods that the light was green at the bottom. I still remember being handed the key to the bathroom vividly. Then again, it's hard to forget when a key is attached to a giant-sized doll taped to a long stick. Good idea, huh?

As we got back on the freeway to head down to Orange County, I was appreciative. How we weren't in a black-and-white heading to jail in the opposite direction made no sense. My body still tingled in relief both physically, having now relieved myself, and mentally. "You seriously didn't check to see if we had gas?" I asked. Atsushi shrugged his shoulders. He lit up a new joint and kept driving. The guy was cool as a cucumber I tell ya.

Windows rolled down, wind whipping my face, I listened to the sound of the motor over Atsushi's reggae music and admired the LA city landscape. "You know, Atsushi, last time I was in jail I got put in a holding cell with a man who only had one arm. He was a gangster Mexican guy and got mad at me for sitting in his spot. How do you have your own spot in a holding cell? Pendejo. You know, I still wonder how did they handcuff that guy. Cops have so much stuff to figure out, man. You ever think about this stuff?"

CHAPTER 21

The Splendors of Budtenders

When we got to the dispensary in Orange County it was like nothing I had ever seen. I had never been in a dispensary before. The women, called budtenders, were all gorgeous. I'd later find out that the owner of the place, Marcus, had hired strippers to work all his stores to help "patients." The dispensary itself was clean and felt very stale. Measures had been made to make the place look like a doctor's office and not a weed shop. All the marijuana was nicely separated, labeled, and served to patients from apothecary jars. It was all very well thought out. In the very back behind closed doors was a big office filled with gun safes. I carried duffle bag after duffle bag into the room to those safes.

As each bag opened, I realized just how much weed we had really brought down. When tallied there were three hundred and ten pounds of weed in the bags. These guys were chill about all of it. It was all a normal day at the office for them. To me it was madness.

"Hey Juan, check this out," Atsushi said. Juan was the second in command at the dispensary. He ran all. Marcus, who I was told owned the place, was a ghost. He was never around. I'd learn that was smart.

Atsushi handed Juan a bag of not any old weed but my weed. Juan smiled and nodded. "Nice," he said. "Big Buddha Cheese. Forty-eight hundred is the ticket," Atsushi nonchalantly told Juan. I had been trying to sell my weed for a while now and hadn't had much success. Juan put all three pounds off to one side. I knew he was going to take it. I now had money for rent and then some.

CHAPTER 22

Count the Money

I'll never forget that day. It changed my life. It gave me direction. It gave me money. It gave me my first real career. I held my head up high; I was a marijuana dealer. You could say it was my "aha" moment.

Slowly, Atsushi tipped me onto all his contacts. He had gone to hundreds of dispensaries and handpicked the ones he thought would be best to work with. What he got out of me was feet on the ground, a place to stay for free, and someone he could trust. What I sold to his contacts was minuscule compared to what he sold to them.

The next week Atsushi drove down again and together we went to go see Juan. Atsushi brought down thirty pounds or so with him this time. Not a lot.

For Atsushi today was another day at work. For me, it was my first paycheck. I looked myself up and down in the mirror and smiled. If it all worked out the way it was supposed to, I'd have a considerable amount of money in my pocket by nightfall. Tim was nervous as well. He didn't say anything to me, but I knew.

You see, these guys didn't pay cash on delivery. Atsushi told me it was all how the business was run. Everything was legal, sort of. While open for business and selling weed to patients, anyone could go get a card and become a patient. Raids of the dispensaries by the cops were common, and to me, it was all like the Wild West. Leaving weight, what we'd call weed, and trusting that you'd be paid at some point was really just a gamble.

I had brought two pounds with me this time. If that worked out, I'd be able to start buying more weed from other guys and selling it to these guys just like Atsushi was doing. It would be a struggle for a while, but I'd build, and I knew I could turn it all into a well-paying job.

When we walked in, Juan paid me what he owed me and took the two pounds. I could tell he was happier to see me than he was Atsushi. I put the money in my pockets. All twenty dollar bills the wads of cash formed two huge bulges in my pants. I felt rich. I sat and waited for Atsushi to handle his business next. While Atsushi chatted with Juan, I thought about how happy Tim would be when I got home. Man, we were we going to party that night.

What Atsushi noticed more than I did, was when we got to the office the couches were filled with turkey bags of weed. I didn't think anything of it. It looked to me like they were doing inventory.

I was more interested in Vanessa, a leggy blond, who was also there in the office. Like all the other women working there, she was really pretty. While I was interested in Vanessa, she wasn't very interested in Atsushi, me, or any of the conversation - really any of any of it. She was racing around opening safes, filling jars, and seemingly keeping very busy. I sat in the corner quietly watching on.

I was certainly not from this world, and I didn't know how any of the cogs worked in the wheel. I was taking it all in and I was intrigued by all of it though. What I was piecing together was that the more I knew, the more money I'd be able to make. So, instead of talking I watched, listened, and learned. The one thing I became certain of was I'd make a lot of money doing all this. Well, until I got caught. I was keenly aware that day would come too. But, how long would that take and how much money could I make before the time came?

"Marcus doesn't want any of this," Juan said. Juan meant ALL the weed on the couches. "Yeah, Juan. So, what do you want me to do with it all?" Atsushi replied. "I don't know. It wasn't selling," Juan told him. What I didn't compute at the time was what that meant was I'd have to carry it all back out of the store and drive it back home in my little Nissan Sentra. On top of all the weed, I also was leaving with over fourteen thousand dollars in cash.

Having cash and weight together is not good. I didn't know that at the time, but I had just got a lot of money, and I sure didn't want to lose it because of anything. I knew that part.

"You know this is bullshit, right?" Atsushi said to Juan. Juan just shrugged his shoulders. "I'm not in charge man," he said. Atsushi looked at Vanessa. She looked back at Atsushi. "I really don't give a fuck either way," she told him. I liked this girl. She had attitude.

After an argument on the phone with Marcus, a final attempt to figure this out, a really pissed-off Atsushi, and I, took all the weed down to my car. Since we didn't know, we were going to have to take all the weed back out of the dispensary, we hadn't brought anything to carry the pounds in. So, we loaded them into black garbage bags that Juan gave us. We filled my trunk, the entire back seat of my car, and some of the front seat with the bags. Walking out of the place I looked like Santa Claus helping out Oscar the Grouch with a move. Atsushi was no longer on crutches but still limping around. I'd say I wasn't happy about driving it all back home, but the truth was it was all still exciting to me.

I drove back home as law-abiding as I could. "Next time count the money," Atsushi said to me over the garbage bags on his lap. I looked over at him. "When you're handed money - count it. Don't trust nobody." That was all he said for a while. Then he started yelling "fuck" and cursing Marcus. I think it had begun to sink in that he was going to have to drive all that weed back to Northern California and deal with some really pissed-off people.

As time went on, I'd change the name on the strain to keep things fresh. OG Cheese was the same as Humboldt Cheese or Stinky Cheese. Stoners think they know weed - they don't. As I grew and began to sell different strains, I'd bring the same turkey bag of weed into the same dispensary a few times and change the name each trip. It almost always worked; they eventually bought it. I learned the business was all about timing and being polite.

It didn't take long 'till I was making money. Lots of money. At home, Tim and I grew weed and in our leisure time, which was most of the time, we'd hang out with the Florida porn star chicks. We'd have huge parties and drink like fish. Life was good. Atsushi would drive down a couple times a week, he and I would go do our rounds, and then we'd all party our asses off.

CHAPTER 23

Dream Sex

My next chapter was to move out and get my own place. It is not that I minded living with Tim. We had a lot of fun. But if I lived in my own house, I could start my own grow and keep all the profit to myself. I could also buy all of Tim's weed, sell that, and make money from that end as well. This was my opportunity to really get going in life. The goal was to build up enough money to invest in something and start making moves. The adage is true. It does take money to make money, and I finally had some money to do something with. My dreams were starting to come true.

Tim had become distant. I tried talking to him but there was something obviously off about him. He wasn't happy. I figured it was because he thought I was leaving him. When he lived with me, I took care of everything. I paid all our bills, handled the grow, and made his life easy. Tim was living the dreams I really had at night - not the G-rated dreams I'd tell my girlfriend that I had had.

Like every guy, I assume, I dreamed of having sex with a hot chick all night. When I woke up, it would be with a fuckin' smile. I wonder now if rock stars dream of wild orgies all night. Did dream sex escalate on how much tail you'd had in your life?

Other than sleep, Tim watched TV all day, smoked weed, drank, and hooked up with porn stars. We were both on different paths, but both destinations were solid.

He had come from a troubled childhood. We all have demons, but he had a lot, and those demons would fight with one another at times. Both of his parents had passed away when he was little, and he had been raised by his aunt and uncle. A great guy we were truly like brothers.   As close as we were, I regret not being able to help him conquer those demons.

CHAPTER 24

Family Time Is Important

One year Tim was invited to his family's house for Easter. This was a big deal. He wasn't used to being invited over to anything family-related. I knew his brothers and sister and so I went with him to the party. Nervous, Tim got drunk fast. His parents, really his uncle and aunt, lived in a nice area. There were beautiful houses with beautiful wives. People would ask themselves how did I get here? And though we pulled up in a large automobile... Tim and I, though we had tried, did not fit in. It may have been because our large automobile, a BMW 5 series, was on the verge of being re-possessed. Our buddy gave it to us to drive until the day came. The car was fast, fun, and a better off-road vehicle than most would think.

Drunk, Tim peeled off his shirt and dove into the pool. What I should have mentioned was Tim's family was Catholic and very religious. The only reason that makes any difference is that drunk Tim forgot he had some unique tattoos. His favorite being a vivid drawing of a clown killing a mime. It was the ultimate murder he'd tell people, "because the mime can't scream for help. Get it?" We'd learn that day that his family's possible non-favorite Tim tattoo was of a skeleton ripping its way out of his back.

When Tim climbed back out of the pool the entire place went quiet. Sisters, brothers, cousins, uncles, aunts, and pastors were all silently saying to themselves (how do I say this nicely?), "Where is that large automobile? This is not my beautiful house" and "this is not my beautiful wife."

To break the mood was me. At first, it was a quiet giggle but as the seconds slowly droned on, I couldn't help but laugh louder and louder. I loved the awkwardness of it all. Tim and I left not too long after that. I never was invited back to that "beautiful" house again.

CHAPTER 25

The Thrills of the Hollywood Hills

In the upcoming weeks I began house hunting for a place I could both live in and grow weed at. I had found a house in the Hollywood Hills that I wanted to rent. I had always wanted to live there because to me living in the hills was a real sign of accomplishment.

There were some problems with the house. The electrical panel was both old and small. That wouldn't work because you need a good amount of power to grow weed. Oh, and then there was the problem that three times a day tourist buses would drive by the house and stop to take pictures. Some positives were that Alicia Silverstone lived next door, the rent was cheap, and it was the Hollywood Hills!

Why did tourist buses drive by you ask? You read the fine print, huh? Hard to get anything by you. Well, some of them came by because the house was haunted. I mean some of them. I don't believe in ghosts though so that wasn't a concern of mine. Did I mention the house was next door to Alicia Silverstone? Don't tell me that wouldn't have been cool.

Alright, fine – I concede. The reason the rent was cheap was because the house was the Wonderland Murder House. It was the site of one of the most famous and gory murder scenes in Los Angeles history. Four people were beaten to death, one person lived with brain trauma, and the whole thing is still a big question mark. An unsolved multiple homicide case. Hence all the ghost stuff. Ghosts only like to hang out where bad shit went down. Just like where aliens only land in the middle of fields in rural America.

We will get into alien stuff later though. Cue the foreshadowing music...

Hear me out. My thoughts had been to grow weed in the house and then film it all. It would make for a great documentary with both the process and the purpose being to calm the spirits down in the home. I would have fun living there, I'd pay my bills growing weed, and I'd have plenty of time to make a cool movie that I could then sell and start an awesome Hollywood career with. Hell, maybe I would even have joined the CSCS. My first film hadn't worked, it didn't make any money, but I thought this one sure would. It's a lot easier to pick who is going to die in a murder movie than to figure out who did it. I'd call the doc. *Stoned to Death*.

It was a great idea and would have been a hell of an experience, but I couldn't swing it. I really needed to focus on making money for now.

CHAPTER 26

Tim

Tim and I both left our party house. I moved into a three-bedroom spot in North Hollywood and Tim moved into his own place not too far away. Whoever had lived in Tim's house had also grown weed. Weed was really taking the valley by storm. It was cool, they had left all their grow trays in the side yard when they moved out. This was a good start. Tim could use those and save a few bucks.

The first night Tim moved into his new house, it got broken into. In the early hours of the morning, they came back into the house, climbed into the attic, and then left. Freaked out, Tim moved in with Pete Peterson.

Tim decided that instead of growing weed at home, he should rent a warehouse and grow there with another friend of ours. Together they had started taking weed to Las Vegas and selling through some guy there. The friend of ours was none other than Pete's mom, the crepe maker. No, I'm kidding it was just a random friend of ours. But wouldn't that have been the "aha" moment that tied the story together?

Warehouses are a different beast. You share walls. That means that the landlord can come into your unit in case of an emergency. That's unfortunately exactly what happened to my friend Tim. Before he had his first harvest a pipe broke in the neighboring unit's wall and flooded the complex. The landlord opened Tim's unit and called the fire department. The fire department then called the police department. After that, you can guess how it all went down. The landlord then went into everyone's unit and found a bunch of other guys growing weed too. On the upside, Tim didn't get into legal trouble because the unit wasn't leased in his name but all the same, he was bummed. Super bummed. Tim's party had ended. A few days later he got real drunk and killed himself.

I had lost my best friend, my brother, the guy who had got me into the business, the guy who had made me feel good about myself. He had been there for me. Yet, I was not there for him. I was train-wrecked.

I buried my heart and kept working. I was determined to make enough money to invest in something that would give me a brighter future. Every night I'd look up to the stars. "Goodnight moon," I'd say aloud. It was to no one, but it made me feel better all the same.

CHAPTER 27

Ant Rants

Atsushi had a cousin. His name was Jin. One night at dinner I asked both of them how they were related. Jin was Korean and Atsushi was Japanese. I learned that they weren't actually related but had grown up in a community where there weren't very many Asian people and so they told everyone they were related. Atsushi said people didn't know the difference anyhow. "There are ants all around my house, but I don't tell people we are related," I told Atsushi. Atsushi ignored me. "How the hell can you tell people you are related when you don't have any family in common and aren't even from the same country? I continued on. "Ants aren't Asian," Atsushi interrupted. "No ants in Asia, dude?" I asked. "We have ants in Korea," Jin interjected. "Atsushi? Ants in Japan?" I asked. "I don't know I've never been there," Atsushi responded.

I liked Jin, or Ox as we called him. He had gotten the nickname when they were in high school because Jin was as dumb as an Ox. He didn't mind the nickname. Maybe he always thought they called him that because of his wide frame and tough exterior. I never asked him.

Ox grew weed, made hash, and had recently begun to make earwax. Earwax had hit the industry by storm. It is a heavily concentrated form of THC, and I couldn't get enough of it to sell. In addition to making literally every kind of weed-related crap there was, Ox had got a job working for a company called Mr. Green.

Mr. Green was a company that made a solvent. The solvent was used when tearing down a NASCAR motor. After every NASCAR race the motor is completely dissembled and then pieced back together for the next race. Jin began bringing empty fifty-five-gallon drums, all labeled Mr. Green, to my house. In the garage, we'd stuff twenty pounds of weed into each one and then weld a fake bottom into the bottom of the drum. No one was the wiser. The drums were then brought back to his work filled with Mr. Green and then transported in the trailers with the NASCARS. It was a perfect way to transport weed throughout the country completely undetected.

CHAPTER 28

Dominoes

Having not taken a vacation in years, I left the country for a couple weeks. The timing was good. I needed to clear my head. I flew to Spain and continued on to France with my mother. It was nice to get away. I get a rush that makes me appreciate life when I travel. The two of us had an awesome trip together. I loved everything about it, but I had a hard time not thinking about all the money I wasn't making because I was away. I knew making money hand over fist in the weed industry would come to an end. I just didn't know when. More and more I thought that day would come sooner than what I was ready for. When that happened, I didn't know how I'd make money. So, I felt like I was being dumb by going on a vacation when things were still good. Still, it is good to spend time with family.

When we got home, it didn't take me long to find out that shit had been crazy. There had been a shooting at Marcus's main spot. The one with all the safes in the backroom. The one I went to most of the time. One of the vendors had been shot in the head while leaving the property. The guy had gotten in his car, and while he was pulling out of the parking lot, he was shot. The guy was fine. The bullet had grazed his head, but it was all a little too close to home for me. I didn't want to die over all this. I just wanted to make enough money to move on to something else and get my life going. The craziest part of it all... Marcus suspected it being an inside job with Juan behind it all.

Under rightful suspicion, Juan had left and opened up a pot store of his own. Atsushi and I supplied him with weed, but I was cautious around the guy. Atsushi didn't seem to care as much. Years later Marcus and Juan would make up even though Juan was responsible for the shooting. Marcus had been right. Life is crazy and weed guys are even crazier. This vacation I took really was the event that marked the beginning of the end.

The first domino to fall belonged to Ox. That may not come as a surprise. The NASCAR thing was a great idea but only lasted for a year or so. Jin had pulled the weed from a barrel and handed it off as planned. The problem wasn't the barrel, the problem was the handing off part. Jin gave it all to some guy who told Jin that he got robbed. When Jin got back to Los Angeles he told me he had gotten screwed. That of course translated to not Jin but me getting screwed. I never got a penny for the weed.

The second domino to fall also belonged to Jin. Jin worked as a chiropractor. He had bought himself a nice house in a nice area. Outside, the house looked just like the one next to it. That house looked like the one next to that. It was suburbia. Safe, quiet, and dull. Inside, Jin's house was anything but like that of his neighbors. Jin had grow lights everywhere. When you went to the bathroom you'd have to maneuver around a light and plants. If you turned on anything in the house you'd blow a breaker. He lived there, but it was madness.

Around this time, the aforementioned earwax started gaining popularity. Earwax is butane hash oil. Making it is dangerous and extremely illegal. So, here is where things get interesting. What is a worse idea than Jin handling, butane, and hash oil? That would have been Jin's mom, butane, and hash oil. Jin had taught his mom how to make earwax, and she would do so in the kitchen of his house. While making it one day she caught the kitchen on fire. She got arrested and was charged with a felony. Figuring that the cops wouldn't come back, Jin quickly set all his lights back up. And that is when Jin's third domino fell. The cops did come back, and this time Jin got charged with a felony. Now Jin was good at figuring. So, you guessed it - he set everything back up again! And sure enough, the cops showed up again. In the end, Jin's mom got house arrest and Jin went to jail for a few years.

CHAPTER 29

A What's Next Fest

That was Jin's last domino, but there were a few more dominoes left in the box. It was inevitable that I too got busted. Jin wasn't the only Ox. The cops had been watching the dispensaries. They watched me come, and then they watched me go. Several unmarked cars followed me, which led to my arrest and an eventual felony charge. At the time I got pulled over I had sixteen pounds of weed on me and a couple thousand dollars. The police were bummed because it wasn't a big haul, and I of course was bummed because I got busted. I'd say we both lost out. The only winner may have been the cop who stole the couple grand. It was taken but never reported as confiscated.

A year or so after being arrested I walked away from it all. What happened to everyone else? Well, Phil is running some other country for Australia, Noah is still trying to make millions of dollars, Jackson wasted most of his millions of dollars on partying, and the rest of the guys still sell weed. Good or bad, when a trade becomes your profession, it's hard to change to doing other stuff. Selling weed isn't exactly a resume builder either. The only one who changed things up was Pete's mom. She stopped making crepes and bought an IHOP. Me, I was ready for something else. I needed another "aha" moment.

JOEL MILLER

BOOK 3

THE FUTURE

CHAPTER 30

So here we are. Me trying to figure out my something else, my "aha" – I was back to where we started. If you remember, I was telling you how I'm tired of being a lemming. Things haven't changed since recounting my life events. I'm still here residing in my one-bedroom air shrine, tired of it all. Yes, residing – not living. That word was intentional. I questioned what could be... no what should be next.

Surrounded by Bert's (remember Bert the old CSCS dude?) Church of Science & Celebrities & Stuff's collection, the answer came to me. You know where you smack yourself in the head real hard and you can't think so good, but then when your brain fully starts working again you are super happy that your head is still attached to your body. That is how it felt. I felt reattached. The venture would be more exciting than everything I had done in the past combined, or it wouldn't work, and I would just be dead unattached from this place.

I had been hitting eBay hard to sell off all of Bert's extensive word collection. In doing so I got more and more amped. If I made enough money on eBay selling this stuff I'd be on my way, and the good news was everything I had was selling like hot crepes.

I listed it all… The collection was massive. Books, audiobooks, DVD's, even tape cassettes, they all ran through eBay's selling platform for pennies on the dollar to spread the word of the church, and more importantly make me a couple bucks. What didn't sell I continued to thumb through. Through hurried readings, because it all sold so fast, I learned of Xemu.

The first time I read about Xemu a light went off. I had a reason for being. My thoughts were simple -not that they are very complicated usually, but what I felt after much studying was that Xemu personified evil. But to me, it was a Dr. Evil kind of evil, not a Mariah Carey evil. There are obviously different types of evil. Mariah Carey is a worse kind. I'll be blunt… her music sucks. And inasmuch she's darn evil I promise you.

I knew about Xemu's evil because all of his dirty shenanigans were well documented in *The Life and Times of Emperor Xemu* book that I had read and then reread when still no one bought it. I wasn't sure why CSters hadn't bought that one. Maybe it didn't have enough words? Either way, it seemed to be mine for the long haul.

What it all meant, the most important part I had taken from the book, was Emperor Xemu knew where the best places to party were. Xemu equated to fun, and I wanted some of that fun. I decided I was going to go to outer space, and it would be Xemu I'd hang out with once I got there!

I wanted to go and check out the universe. To be like Spock without the ears. Remember how I told you I'd look up at the stars and then wonder what was next? Well one day those twinkly bastards answered. Subtle twinkles. Each an invitation. Xemu…

Space… knocking boots with an alien hot chick, the universe, and beyond.

Getting to space would all take time and so I began to research and plan. At least I now knew what was next for me. I had always been searching for what I was really meant to do. The answer now rested within the literal pages of destiny. Outer space, the worlds beyond quickly became a better ideal than the COVID-ridden world that I belonged to. "Belonged to," why even say that? Maybe I never belonged here at all.

Armed with *The Life and Times of Emperor Xemu*, I decided to plot how to get onboard Elon Musk's space shuttle.

I knew Jeff Bezos also had a space shuttle, but hear me out. What if Bezos was actually Xemu? If Xemu was living on Earth, I figured he'd look like that little Bezos fucker. I knew if Bezos was Xemu we'd never get along. I couldn't take that chance. Now, most of the time I didn't think Bezos was Xemu. Maybe here and there… I'd ponder it. I mean I'm not crazy or anything. I just also figured Bezos probably had his shuttle built by Temu or maybe some guy who had been fired from Temu. He was always after a deal that weasel. I wanted to get there. Not be blown up trying to get there. I hated Amazon. Bezos was too much of a corporate asshole and to be frank, honest, he was just too smart for me. Remember, I told you I'm not crazy or anything.

A complete tangent here, but who was this Frank guy that became synonymous with being honest. I'll bet that guy was a prick too.

Now, Musk was different. He made cool stuff. He was a maker of not just kids. He made cars for kids that adults drove. He was a mover, a shaker, a true innovator. And because he was so busy taking care of all those kids, I'd bet his security sucked balls. That's what I was hoping for at least.

Let's try to stay on track here, back to Xemu. I don't know how we got sidetracked by Musk's ball-sucking. I knew Elon Musk could never be Xemu, because as a true Musk fan, or what I like to call a Musketeer, I remember when he publicly stated that he was afraid of artificial intelligence. The scriptures of Xemu are filled with people who are not just mostly composed of artificial intelligence but are also proud to include in their artificial repertoire the addition of artificial lips, hips, breasts, and derrieres. They are indeed almost one hundred percent artificial. There was nothing artificial about Xemu, though.

CHAPTER 31

✓ **Check**

Artificial intelligence and all that other stuff aside, there were other reasons I chose to steal Musk's shuttle over Bezos's shuttle. The no-playing-around fact of the matter was I bought stuff on Amazon. I know I said I hated the site a bit ago but if I got caught and then banned from buying on Amazon, where would I buy my Gustaf's licorice allsorts? Gustaf's licorice allsorts were an important part of my life. You see, it's hard to find fresh ones in the United States. I wasn't prepared to take any risk that would compromise that. To further separate Musk from Bezos. If Musk banned me from Twitter, or whatever the hell he renamed it, I didn't care.

Last but not least - in fact very far from last but not least - years earlier I had kind of got to know Musk's sister a bit. I was out on the Sunset Strip in Los Angeles with a bunch of Australian friends. I was probably with Phil, my consul general buddy.

Many of the bars on the world famous Sunset Strip are just that – world famous. We had picked a bar that was not so world-famous. It was actually a hole in the wall dumpy little building with cheap beer. Having a good ol' time, I got to chatting to a girl who was friends with the Aussie crew. After a bit of idle chit-chat, I asked her what kind of work she did. Her answer, "I work for a man named Schmuhl Smallowitz." That silenced me quick. Not that I expect anyone to know who Schmuhl Smallowitz is, but you see I sure did. Well, I knew the name. I smiled at her awkwardly. "A good Jewish name. I am working with Sven Smallowitz right now," I told her. "Oh," she replied. It wasn't an excited "oh" but rather an awkward "oh."

"Can I buy you a drink?" I asked her to change the mood. "Sure," she replied clearly also agreeing that it may be smart to change the topic. This banter was all an easy way to say to one another, "what do we care who we work for."

Schmuhl and Sven Smallowitz were brothers. They had written and produced some big films together. *Bobbing for Bunnies, Genocide Sucks, The Cutest Hurricane in Ecuador, The Cutest Hurricane in Ecuador II,* and one of my favorite films *Liberals Hunt Endangered Everything.* While their films had been great box office successes, they DID NOT like one another. Schmuhl and Sven had stopped working together years earlier and I don't think it had been a fun separation. I had even been told they made hamantaschen separately now. The Smallowitz family had met up for generations to make hamantaschen together, so that was of course sad.

The brothers were now etched amongst great brothers who no longer spoke to one another. Adolf Dassler & Rudolf Dassler (founders of Puma & Adidas), Don Everly & Phil Everly (The Everly Brothers), Liam & Noel Gallagher (Oasis), and of course Lyle & Erik Menendez (Brothers from the super successful Netflix show Monsters), to name a few.

So, what did this all have to do with Elon Musk? Just like this bar was second fiddle to all the other bars on Sunset and perhaps all the other bars in Los Angeles, Elon's sister was second fiddle to her older brother. But second fiddle is still classy to a guy like me. I'm a second-fiddle kind of guy. It was short-lived, but I had hung out with the family.

So, in summation the way I figured it all was:
   A. I bought my stuff, licorice, through Bezos's company.
   B. I could call Musk's sister and remind her I bought her a drink long ago, and maybe she'd talk her brother into not cutting my wiener off if I got caught stealing his

shuttle.

C. If Bezos was Xemu then I'd find something cooler for me to do in space. I already knew Musk wasn't.

✓ Check Mark Elon!

CHAPTER 32

Finders Keepers, Elon

And so, with all the important design now in place, I began to research. It was hard to research Xemu. They really needed to write more books on him. Maybe that's what I'd do. Write a series of books so people could get to know him better. *Xemu and Friends Play Kickball, Xemu and Friends at the Titty Bar, Xemu Pulls My Finger, Xemu Offers Romantic Advice for Couples Over the Age of Sixty-Five.*

Alas, I had no answers. There was nothing on the guy. What language would Xemu speak? Would he be my friend? Could he be a friend? Did he even like pickleball? Of course, he did. The game is awesome, but would he pull my finger? I didn't know. I knew for sure I would wear black when I met him though. Wearing black of course, always helps things.

While all these matters were important there were other concerns that were more pressing. How would I get into the spaceship? What should I bring with me to space? How the hell do you drive a spaceship?

Maybe, if I could talk to Musk, he too would want to go find Xemu? While I figured he would - I also figured it would be harder to meet Musk, have a conversation with him, and *then* steal his space shuttle. Deduction prevailed - It would be easier to steal it under the radar. So, with these variables in mind, I harnessed my thoughts to pull off the theft of the century.

After a couple months of thinking about these factoring questions and other strategic plannings, what I had sorted out was that it would be easier to steal the space shuttle if they launched it out of California. I know what you are thinking. Is that the only thing you sorted out? That is your strategic planning? I'll tell you this - nothing about space travel is easy to figure out and I am not good at planning things. So, back off!

However, what I did know was that if they launched the shuttle out of Florida, I wasn't sure I'd have the gas money to get there. If I couldn't get there – then there was no mission. That part I knew.

CHAPTER 33

Captain 'Merica

As luck would have it sure enough the next launch was going to be in my state. The great state of California that is. That meant that the shuttle was going to be stored in California as well. I smiled from ear to ear when I read the news. It was all meant to be. But when would be the ideal day to steal it? There had to be a day, a perfect time of year, a time when important planets aligned. There's a moment for everything. I needed to figure out that perfect moment to steal a space shuttle.

Again, meant to be, as luck would have it, a Comic-Con was coming up soon in San Diego. Better yet... Comic-Con was featuring an exclusive pre-screening of the next *Captain America* movie. I knew no one would show up to work at SpaceX that day!

Now guys with tiny penises are notorious for buying big trucks. Those small-cocked bastards also yield good ol' firepower. Is this yet another tangent? No, far from it actually. The thought may make people shutter, but this was my life I was trying to protect here. Elon Musk must have the smallest cock of all to build a freakin' space shuttle. That would mean his minions would surely harness A LOT of firepower.

To further the problem in that I had a regular-size willie - I had no firepower. I had seen *The Untouchables*, and I remembered when Sean Connery told that guy not to bring a knife to a gunfight. That was about the extent of my tough-guy abilities. If you watched the movie, it was the extent of that guys too.

What it all came down to was I had to be creative. I knew I was. It truly is one of my superpowers. But I couldn't rely on only being creative. I also had to be sneaky. Very sneaky.

I continued on. Keeping my plans to myself, I researched. If anyone had known what I was up to they would have said I was very focused. But again, I was learning the fine skill of being sneaky. I had a ton of things to remember, but I didn't want to forget to torrent the new *Captain America* movie. I kept having to remind myself of that. I too was going to miss Comic-Con and like Elon Musk's fire-powered militants, I didn't want to miss the movie.

CHAPTER 34

Ciao Bella

Who would I say bye to? I knew my plan was a little outlandish, some would say even a bit absurd. I wasn't crazy though, and I didn't want to hear that kind of crap from anybody. I was determined to make Outer Space happen, but I also wasn't afraid to be realistic about it all. There was a good chance I wouldn't see anyone I knew again. So, the real question - did I care?

I'd fail. If that happened, I'd either go to jail forever, be killed off, or I would succeed and never come back to Earth again. All those scenarios meant that saying goodbye had meaning. It was really going to be a genuine goodbye. I thought, who should I say bye to and what to say to them? I contemplated meeting up with Mary Sue. But to be honest with myself, It would be more of an attempt for a last fling than really saying goodbye. I opted against that. She had a new fella in her life and the chances of me getting any seemed slim to none. The dude was in pretty good shape.

Ring... Ring... Yeah, I called Mary Sue. It was worth a try. She picked up, "Yep." "Hey Mary Sue, how the heck are ya'?" I said trying to sound fun and positive. "I said ya' Steve. That means what do you want? Spit it out. I am right in the middle of stuff," she replied.

I continued on hesitantly. "I wanted to let you know I'm leaving. It's a five-year mission: to explore strange new worlds, to seek out new life and new civilizations, and to boldly go where no man has gone before."

I could hear her talking to someone else in the background. "This fuckin' dumbass is seriously reciting the intro to Star Trek to me in a pathetic attempt to get laid. This is the imbecile I was with before you and now I'm here with you. Aren't I lucky? The world is filled with freakin' blessings isn't it, Bill. Yeah, you can keep ignoring me. I'm being condescending. Do you even know what that means, you worthless meathead asshole?" Mary Sue turned back to focus her undivided attention at me.

"Did I call at a bad time?" I asked. "Steve, I hope you have a great trip. Is there anything else you need?" she replied.

"I was hoping to see you again. I don't think I'm coming back," I said. "Steve, let's cut the shit. I'm not fucking you and I really don't care where you are going. Anything else?"

"A blowjob," I asked. The phone went quiet for a moment. "Is that a serious question," she asked. "Well, yeah kind of was," I laughed uneasily.

"You worthless scumbag, two-bit, piece of human excrement. You seriously think I would ever..." I hung up the phone. My guess was she kept cussing me out for a few more minutes before she realized I was even gone. Women are like an amusement park run by a terrorist.

Who else should I say bye to? Calling Mary Sue hadn't gone so well, and I couldn't think of anyone else. Maybe, I should just go on my way and not say anything to anybody. The problem was I wanted to tell someone. I guess it was the extrovert in me. You can tell a lot about whether a plan is dumb or not by reading the other guys reaction. I decided to reveal all to my Scottish neighbor Davey. Davey was pretty much the closest thing to a friend I had.

My relationship with Davey began and ended the same way each week. I would take Davey's garbage cans to the curb when he was too drunk to remember, which was every week. In return, Davey would mumble niceties over the wall to me whenever he saw me. I never knew what he was saying, but all in the way he mumbled his words, I knew we were on great terms.

Head held high, I walked over and knocked on Davey's door. I had never knocked on his door before. Though his car was there, no one answered. I rang the door chime. Through the door, I could hear an automated voice: "Oy, some asshole is at the door." While pondering where and how Davey got such a cool doorbell the door opened.

All other questions I may have had became irrelevant. "Where did you get the doorbell?" I asked. "Wife bought it on Etsy," he told me. I had never seen anyone else at Davey's house. "You have a wife?" I asked. "Ay, lives in Scotland. It's why we get on so good," he told me. "They have Etsy all the way in Scotland?" I asked. Davey clarified, "She lives in Houston, Scotland. And so, I moved to Houston, Texas. We figured it would work out better that way. Issue was Houston, Texas is a shithole. So, I moved here instead. She still thinks I live in Texas though. So don't fuckin' tell her." He looked at me sternly. "Oh, I wouldn't dream of doing that," I replied.

I handed Davey a bottle of Scotch. "Here this is for you," I said. "How do you know I drink Scotch?" he asked. "I've been told it's what most people drink in Houston." "That's true," he replied.

"I need something, Davey," I continued on. Davey nodded. "I'm going to steal a space shuttle, and I need firepower. As I see it a fella who has a space shuttle would have a lot of firepower, and I have none."

I was waiting for Davey to invite me in, but he didn't. I stood on one side of the threshold, and he stood on the other. It was clear we were both evaluating the situation. "A man who would build a fucking space shuttle would certainly have a small tadger," he finally said to me. "Right, that is what I was thinking," I happily agreed. The ice had been broken. Davey reached over to a cupboard that stood next to the front door. He pulled out a pink gun and lovingly wiped his hand over it. He looked up at me and

I instinctively put my hands up in the air. "I'm not going to shoot you. You idiot," he blurted out. Embarrassed, I hurriedly put my arms down by my sides again. Davey handed me the gun. I hadn't noticed when it was pointed at me, but the grips of the gun had Hello Kitty caricatures on them. "Where did you get this gun, Davey?" I asked. "Etsy" he replied. "I'm not going to give you any bullets though. Don't want you hurting yourself. Bring me back a moonrock."

Davey closed the front door, and I walked back towards my house. On my way home I grabbed a rock off the ground. If things didn't go well, I could always give the rock to Davey.

CHAPTER 35

Signs

The drive from Los Angeles to San Diego is just under three hours. It gave me time to realize just how ill-prepared my plan really was. There wasn't a lot online about how to drive/fly the SpaceX beast. I knew I wasn't even very good at driving my own car. I had been pulled over from everything to driving too slow in the slow lane, to driving too fast in the fast lane, the common bust of my lights not working, and when I was a kid running illegal lights underneath my car. I knew they were wrong, but they sure looked cool. I'd had a ticket for everything.

On the way down to San Diego coming from Los Angeles, there is a famous sign on the side of the freeway that all Southern Californians know. It is a huge sign with a family running. The sign is meant to deter drivers from hitting people illegally crossing the border. Just like long-distance runners, the family on the sign wore no headphones. Why would you travel that far on foot and not listen to music or a podcast or something? I continued to drive on, but I kept thinking about the sign. I wondered how many people had been mowed over on the freeway before the sign was constructed. I also thought how the sign wouldn't be all that effective in Outer Space. There would be nowhere to post a sign and yet theoretically aliens could still run into another spaceship. I wondered how many aliens, illegal or not, got hit while cruising around both down here and up there.

I'd bet there were no rules in space though. If you get into a space shuttle accident up in space did anyone care? Who paid for the damage to the ship? The time passed quickly while I ran all these space scenarios through my brain.

Before I knew it, I was at a guard gate. Off in the distance, I could see the space shuttle. I was close. "What you want?" the man at the guard gate asked, jogging me back to reality. "I'm here to see Xemu," I told him. "No one really here today. They are all at that Comic-Con thing," he flippantly told me. "Yeah, I can see that being a thing too," I told him. Was I broing out with this guy? We were off to a good start. "Know where you are going?" He asked. "Yeah, sure" I replied. The gate opened and he waved me through. I drove on confidently. I reminded myself I had to continue to be sneaky. Very sneaky. I was off to a good start.

Driving through the compound there were signs everywhere. Who knew people would need to do so many things here other than fly a spaceship? I didn't read the signs. There was no real point. I could see the space shuttle not too far off and that is where I needed to be. I pulled into a parking spot that had my favorite signage thus far. It read "Tesla Parking Only – Elon Musk." I wondered what would be said about the oil stain my van would be leaving in the spot.

I had purchased a vest to look more like a man of authority. Across the back of what I received read "Service Dog." What I had ordered was an Amazon police vest. That vest had really looked pretty darn official. However, what I got from Amazon was the wrong vest. Now, instead of a cop, I was a service dog. Normally, I would have complained to Amazon and got another one sent to me for free but there was no time to wait for the correct vest this time. I had to get to the shuttle before Comic-Con was over. I was just glad they hadn't sent me a tutu. I think a tutu emblazoned with the words "Service Dancer" wouldn't have worked so good.

The service dog vest wasn't perfect, but it was the best I could do on such short notice. On the upside, service dog people have been getting away with murder for years now. I knew all those dogs weren't service pets. We all knew! But when nobody wants to deal with something, shit just passes through. I hoped to be like fiber cruising through the lower intestine.

I put on my vest and zipped it up. It felt snug and I smiled as I gained some undeserved confidence. DING! The eBay sound on my phone rang and it totally freaked me out. I unzipped my vest again and took a look at my phone. I had just sold *The Life and Times of Emperor Xemu* book. "Little late there, CSter dude," I laughed aloud. I wouldn't be sending that out, that was for sure.

"Sir," I heard a male voice say. I turned around. "You not hear me?" he asked. "Honestly, my hearing is pretty bad," I told him. "Age - it's a son of a bitch. Ain't it?" He replied. I laughed a little. "Yeah." He pulled out a little black book and a pen. "Name," he asked me. "Barf Candy," I blurted out. "Excuse me," he said. "Shit, that wasn't very sneaky," I said to myself.

I had been thinking about John Candy in *Spaceballs*. I think it was because of my slick Amazon service dog apparel. It wasn't the smartest thing I could have said but it just kind of came out. With my left hand, I felt inside my jacket to make sure my Hello Kitty gun was still on my person. This could go poorly.

"Bartholomew Candy. It's an English name," I said to him. "That's a long fuckin' name, man. I'd go by Barf or Bart or whatever too," he said. The man closed the book without writing in it. "I'm supposed to log people into a computer, but it's just such a bitch," he went on to say. I nodded and kept walking down the corridor towards the shuttle. This was perfect. So far there was no record of me ever being here.

I had been keeping it cool, and I was confident that that was what had got me this far. But one thing I'm good at is praising myself and then immediately doubting everything I just praised myself about.

I could read the headline now. Some guy broke into SpaceX pretending to be Barf from *Spaceballs* with a Hello Kitty pistol. Maybe that was a bad idea. What kind of a service dog would use a gun emblazoned by a loveable cat? It's that kind of crap that... No, wait a minute. I gotta focus. I gotta stay fucking SNEAKY. I was getting sidetracked.

Whatever I had been thinking about didn't matter anymore. It had worked. There before me was the door to the space shuttle. I looked on at it thinking, "Now what." Not for long though. I'll tell you that. I walked my dumb ass into that space shuttle with a huge grin. I'd made it. I had really made it. I was one sneaky mother fucker after all.

CHAPTER 36

Mommy Dearest

The entry to the shuttle was like a birth canal to Elon Musk's life. Riveted to the walls were photos of Elon Musk and family. I didn't have time to really look at all of them but wondered if he lived in this thing. Everything inside the shuttle was simple but plush. No one was anywhere. I walked into the cockpit and sat down in the captain's chair. It was as it looked, comfy. There was only one button on the entire console. Lettered above it read "Push this to go." Across the bottom of the console read "Powered by Tesla (of course.)" Cocky SOB, wasn't he? I looked around for a space suit. I'd need that.

Finding a space suit proved to be harder than I thought it would be. I didn't know how long Comic-Con lasted and my brain started racing again. I began to panic. I went from level to level looking for a room with a space suit. There was a kitchen. There was a lounge. There was a bathroom. But where the hell did Elon keep his space suits?!

I needed to buy some time. Walking back through Elon's birth canal I pushed a button at the main door labeled "Close Sesame." The huge heavy door closed softly. Fairly confident that would set off alarms but also hopefully keep people out, I rushed back to the control room.

I was now totally tripping out. I couldn't find the fucking space suit. I went back to the cockpit room thinking this was the ultimate security device. I couldn't go up into space without a space suit. I resolved myself to just sit there until I got busted. I put my head down between my legs and clasped my hands over my head. It's a good stretch and it always chills me out. I had done yoga for years and it's one of the stretches I remember fondly. With my head down below the console, I noticed a single red button. It had no markings on it. To me, it looked like an "Oh shit" button. I figured if they were going to come and bust me, I might as well hurry up the process. I pushed the red button, and a nude photo dropped down from the bottom of the console.

I did not recognize this woman, but the nipples in the photo were buttons. I pushed the left nipple and over a speaker, I heard a sultry woman: "Momma loves you, Elon." Was this woman Elon's mother? I'd have to go look at the photos in the birth canal entry later.

A red light highlighted what looked like a closet behind me. I stood up and walked over to it. Standing in front of what I hoped was a door, I saw myself in the reflection. Looking on at myself I knew I didn't have time for this, but I couldn't help but look at who was looking back at me. I should have been proud of myself. What a feat to get this far. But I didn't think that. I felt nervous. This was cool stuff going on, and I still felt kind of like a loser.

"Good morning, Elon. Who's the most important person in human history?" the speaker asked. I stood there for a moment wondering what was next. It was time for me to snap out of it. "Oh, Elon are you having a rough morning, Pumpkin? It's OK my darling. I'll wait for you. Who's the most important person in human history?" the speaker asked again. I didn't know what to say or do. It was clearly a security system set off by voice recognition. "Reset," I said firmly. "Sure. What would you like for the new password to be?" the speaker asked. "Barf Candy," I replied. There was a pause. "Are you sure?" the speaker asked. "Yes, yep - that's it," I responded. "Password reset in progress. Long live SpaceX and may Tesla continue to drive you to your happy place." Those were nice words. I deserved to find my happy place, I thought.

"Good morning blank. What is the new password?" the speaker asked. "Barf Candy," I re-stated. I answered more as a question than a reply. I wasn't sure what was going on.

Watching on, a closet opened, and a space suit appeared before my eyes. The suit looked like the Marvel Iron Man outfit, but instead of red it was a polished raw steel. It was bitchin'.

Inside the closet was another photo of the same woman that had popped out from under the console before. This time I pushed her right nipple. "Momma likes that," the speaker said. The entire suit opened. I stepped into it and once standing inside, the back snapped back closed once again. It fit like a glove. Not an OJ Simpson glove either. A nice fitting one. *Captain America* screening my ass. This was way cooler. Now where was the helmet for this thing? I looked at each nude photo. The nipples were now all flashing red, and her lips turned from silver to blue. I put my finger on the lips. Nothing happened. "Now don't be shy, Pumpkin," the sultry voice said. I bent over and licked the photo on the lips. The lips turned to a solid silver. "Your favorite color - mercury silver metallic," the speaker said. This was a peculiar security system.

A cabinet opened and there before me lay Elon's helmet. The helmet shined metallic green and was shaped like Kermit the Frog. I put the helmet on and both doors closed back up. I thought our mirrored closet door was pretty slick, but this system trumped anything Tim and I had put together.

Next, I once again sat down in the pilot's chair. The cabin door sealed. "Getting ready for liftoff. All doors sealed. Let's do this. Bezos is your bitch you stud!" The shuttle began to shutter.

The Kermit eyes glowed and the song "Mr. Big Stuff" began to play. Everything around me roared loudly. The song faded into oblivion as the engines hummed louder and louder. Once at what must be maximum decibel, they got even louder.

I'd say I wondered what the headlines would be now, but truthfully things were so chaotic I wasn't thinking about that. If anything, I was hyper-focused on if I was going to implode. I recited "Earth below us drifting, falling, floating, weightless..." over and over again in my head as a settling mantra. Fuck being sneaky. This was intense.

Roughly eight and a half minutes later, things suddenly chilled out. Looking out the large window I was now in Earth's Orbit. I had made it. Not just made it. I had made it, alive. Now what?

CHAPTER 37

Elon's Favorite Book

I hadn't taken into account food and water. I had remembered to bring my wallet and phone, though I wasn't quite sure why I had. It's not like I could go back now even if I wanted to. While The shuttle seemed to be on course, I wasn't sure if I was simply drifting through space or if there was in fact a destination that had been pre-set.

I decided the most efficient way to spend my time would be to walk around the shuttle to check out my new home and find something to eat and drink. Looking around a lounge-type room it was abundantly obvious this place was way nicer than my house. "I could totally live here," I said aloud to nobody.

I sat down on what I'd soon find to be a cushy sofa and gazed around the room. The room's walls were filled with books. It sure was quiet in here. Standing back up, I walked over to one of the bookcases. The books all appeared to be prioritized by binding color rather than organized in any sort of alphabetical order. Furthermore, the entire section was filled with memoirs, bios, and autobiographies only. Not a single book on The Church of Science & Celebrities & Stuff, I thought. On the bottom shelf was one book all by its lonesome. The book had been earmarked many times and when I flicked through the many pages there were highlighter and notes on many a page. This must be Elon's favorite book. I read the title out loud to myself, *Memoir of a Roadie*. What a great title.

There it was again! I jumped around and out of the corner of my eye, I saw her. I knew someone had been watching me! Who was it though? What I had seen was an African American female who couldn't have been more than 2 feet tall. Her skin - soft and shiny, but her eyes looked unhuman. I could only describe them as ones looking like those that would belong to a lemming. [I know there is a lot of lemming talk in this story. It's turning into almost a Wikipedia on lemmings. Here's the deal. When I got to space, I'd have no idea that aliens had lemming eyes. If I had known, I would have started the story with some other animal. "I was tired of being a dolphin. Fuck dolphins," something like that instead. But these aliens didn't have dolphin eyes, they had lemming eyes. Life throws you curveballs.

It had all been so fast, but she had been wearing what appeared to be a baby's onesie. Elon's favorite book in hand, I ran after the little lady.

Nowhere for her to really go - I knew I'd find her. I wasn't scared or anything like that. I mean, I had made it this far and she was 24 inches tall. Luck was certainly on my si... From out of nowhere the little onesie-wearing two-foot-tall fucked up eye bitch grabbed onto my leg. Punched me in the balls, climbed onto my back, and wailed on my head until I passed out. The last thing I remember was dropping the book on the first ball kick and then at some point screaming out in agonizing pain, "You little midget cunt."

CHAPTER 38

Can't We All Get Along

When I came to, I was lying back on the couch. I looked around but no one was to be seen. My head hurt like hell, that was for sure. Sitting upright, I put my head down in my open palms. Do they have ice in space? Before me stood a seven-foot-tall ghost white man with the same lemming eyes as the two-foot-tall bitch. "Not going to tie me up?" I asked. "I don't think handling you if need be is a problem at this point," he replied. I grimaced and leaned back.

"I used to be tough," I told him. I had honestly never been tough. "Where's your little friend?" I asked. "We are always together. We are one." I looked around but didn't see her. "So, you are a they/them. That's kind of the in thing right now. I get it. Anyone else on the ship or just you two?" I asked. "Again, the midget cunt and I are one. There are no other life forms on this vessel though to answer your question."

"Can we agree that was my initiation, and now we can be civil to one another?" I asked. "Yes," he replied. His response was flippant; I wasn't sure if it was a sincere answer or not. I suppose I wasn't certain if I had asked a sincere question either. So, the reply made sense.

"Now what?" For the next few minutes, we sat quietly. I say "we" because there were two of us... or maybe a group of us. A they/them of us? Whatever you want to call it, I sat and waited.

"Since I think we may spend a bit of time together, what do you want me to call you?" I asked. "I'm Frick, my friend I call Frack," he said. "OK, that's cute," I blurted out while laughing to myself. I extended my hand to shake the group of long phalanges Frick had at the end of an overextended pale arm. Frick really didn't know how to handle that. He cocked his head to the left and then to the right. As his arm extended, his alien-type fingers crept their way up my arm. Frack came out of the shadows. She didn't do anything other than watch on. In an incredibly quick moment, the fingers retracted back to Frick's person. The room sat quiet.

"Well, that was fuckin' weird," I said. "You didn't ask what to call me?" I asked. "Would you prefer Steve or Barf Candy?" Frick asked me. How did he know that?

I didn't want to ask. I wanted to appear like I knew more than I really did. If I asked, I feared it would make me look like an inferior being.

"Steve works. That is what my mom named me," I said. Frack nodded approval. It was the first sign of any form of acceptance by either one of them. "Mom," Frick said. It wasn't a question nor a comment. It seemed more like a mental checkmark. I guess you'd call it an observation. "Actually, call me Mark Zuckerberg," I said. "No," was all Frick replied. Did he know Zuckerberg too? What was with all these billionaire guys knowing aliens?

"Elon didn't send you," Frick stated. "Might have! Why you think that?" I asked.

I knew darn well why. One look at me and it was pretty clear. When I dressed to leave the house, I should have thought longer about what to wear in space. Under my service dog apparel was a U2 shirt. David Bowie would have been cooler, but the Bowie shirts were a lot more expensive at Hot Topic and I couldn't afford one. It sucks being broke. Now I risked an alien's first introduction to music from Earth being a band I thought wasn't that great. I also kind of smelled. Why is it that if you don't wash a brand new shirt you get BO wearing it faster than with an old crusty hand-me-down shirt?

"So, what do you and Elon talk about?" I blurted out. It was time to break the ice with these/ them people. Both Frick and Frack stayed quiet for an uncomfortable amount of time. "Frack doesn't say much, huh," I said. This was awful. I would have never thought that aliens would have such horrible social skills.

"Why are you here, Steven?" Frick asked. "No, me first. What do you and Elon talk about?" I asked again. Again, no one answered me. "I asked first," I continued on.

It's not like I really cared what they talked about, but I had to build a bridge of some sort with these anti-social pricks.

"Blastar," Frack spoke out. I looked down at her. "I was under the impression you couldn't speak," I told her while nodding approval. I was a bit surprised. It had worked. I had actually broken some ground. "Fucking Blastar. That's what I'm talking about," I replied. I had no idea what Blastar is or was but I had gotten my way. I was happy about that. "It's a game. We like it," Frack further filled me in. "Good to know," I said.

"Why are you here, Steven?" Frick asked me again. He stated his question in such a way that it was clear he thought it was exceedingly more important than my question had been.

CHAPTER 39

Matcha Tea

Why was I there? Where was there? I may as well have offed myself. It certainly would have been easier to drink a couple of beers, smoke a joint, and then crash out for good. Instead, I got this hair-brained idea. What's even more ridiculous was it had worked.

"I was sent here to recruit alien strippers for shoe modeling positions throughout a place called Texas," I told them. "We like Buc-ees beef jerky," Frack said. Frack didn't speak too often but I sure liked what she had to say when she did. "It's an awesome place. There's no doubt about it," I replied. Frack nodded her approval..

"Look, you two seem cool. Even though you unnecessarily just kicked my fucking ass, Crack. Oh shit, I meant Frack. Sorry, Frack not Crack." Frack blinked a couple of times but didn't show any reaction otherwise. "I came up here because I want to find this Xemu guy," I said.

I would have had no way of knowing it, but that was the wrong thing to say. The very worst thing. Frick moved his tentacle arms up from his sides. The blue hue of his skin began to turn a red/purple color. More tentacles crawled out of his pant legs and spread throughout the room.

"Xemu," he said in a deep bloodcurdling tone. For the first time, Frick became ominous. I figured this would be a good time to go make a cup of tea. I got up and left the room. No one, or thing, followed me. That was good.

The kitchen was simple. No magnets on the fridge or anything. Opening up a cupboard it was filled with Diet Coke. I was so thirsty. Diet Coke was not my go-to, but I had to drink something. I cracked the can open and downed the delicious liquid. The belch I let out was a stomach primal scream. I didn't like soda, but I sure did like that part of it all. What I really needed was a cup of tea though. I began taking things out of the cabinets in hopes of finding a bag or two.

Not noticing, red tentacles had been filling the floor and walls around me. As I reached towards a second can of Diet Coke a tentacle wrapped around me, flinging me around.

"Man, I just wanted some damn Matcha tea, man. Is that really too much to ask?" I pleaded. The tentacles dragged me into the main room again. "You are full of fucking surprises, aren't you? You are a Cthulhu now. That's cute. Watch the freakin' hair Frick," I barked out. It wasn't like I knew where to find a barber up here. "Xemu!" Frick angrily screamed aloud.

My brain rushed as the tentacles tightened around me. "Xemu!" Frick repeated. On the other side of the room, I could see Frack horrified. Her soft skin turned leathery before my eyes. I watched on as her very life was sucked right out of her. Frick blew space air in my face and my eyes fell asleep. My brain rushed with information. Horrible information. So much information. Frick had done terrible things in his lifetime, and I was now witnessing each of them. Mass genocides of armies, destruction of entire planets, tearing innocents from limb to limb, cannibalizing pregnant women. In every sequence that scattered through my mind, Frick stood emotionless and tall. Committing these atrocities had no effect on him. They were who he was. Last in line... I saw none other than Frack.

Through Frick's eyes, I saw Frack destroy her entire village. Under the cloak of night, she traveled from tent to tent, each time with more blood on her hands than the time just before. I watched on -

her village burning in the distance, everyone dead, while Frick and Frack walked away.

Moments later I was back on the shuttle, panic-driven, and gasping for air. Looking around at my surroundings, everything seemed to be back to normal. If you'd call being in a stolen space shuttle with two maniacal aliens normal. Frick stood before me, once again a purple hue. There was something different now though. It was the strangest phenomenon. I could hear Frick's thoughts and, odder, yet it was almost like I expected to be able to now do so. Like I had always been able to read minds I just hadn't bothered. For the first time in my life, I felt like a sentient being.

"Why Frick?" I asked. Frick and I were mentally one. I could hear him, and he in turn could hear me. All without the unnecessary use of vocalization. In addition, as I now knew everything about him, he knew everything about me. Exploring through Frick's fractured mind I had so many questions. He had lived what seemed like hundreds of years. Perhaps thousands of years. As more and more memories rushed through, I became more confused. Why never change? Why such hatred?

Frick answered my questions. "We are they/them," Frick said to me. In the corner was a deceased Frack. I had now taken her place. "We are they/them?" I questioned back.

Space blew ass. What the fuck was I going to do now?

CHAPTER 40

Candied Nuts or Deviled Donuts?

Have you ever gone to the donut shop to buy the chocolate bar and all they had left was the round sprinkle donut? You felt slighted, right? I had got sprinkle donuted by this alien bastard.

The worst part of it wasn't constantly re-living the murders nor even the pillaging. It was Frick's shitty food pleasures. Frick had horrible taste in food. Why couldn't he dream of warm brownies, deviled eggs, and ice cream like everyone else? It was one thing to share the same thoughts, but a total other thing to share the same food interests. It was like I had gotten married to a five-year-old boy who kept getting busted trying to eat the dog's food. Not even the good dog food but the cheap wet kind.

While Frick kept trying to persuade me to change my mind, I kept trying to persuade him to think about Denver omelets and Brussels sprouts instead. I don't know why I love Brussels sprouts, but I had greatly missed them while up in space circling the Earth. These mental wars went on for what must have been a couple of days with neither Frick nor myself thinking about much of anything else other than food. Neither one of us ever convinced the other to be more open to trying different delicacies either. I knew – we were one- but there seemed to be no middle ground here. Answering my thoughts back Frick predictably said, "We are one."

"Shut up, you sprinkle donut," I replied.

CHAPTER 41

Memories of Xemu – A Love Story

I mention circling the Earth. But was that in fact what we were doing? Breaking communication with Frick about whether eating human intestines tasted better than tuna tartare I asked the more important question, "Hey Frick, where are we headed? All I've seen is space for days now. It's been space for days... weeks... I don't even know. This is super boring. It's like driving through Kansas a few hundred times in a row."

I assumed Frick was guiding this thing. He was the alien and not me. This was his home. I was just a visitor. Like a glimmering page in a book, Frick revealed something new.

I saw myself at a raging party sifting through various aliens chatting it up and having what seemed like wonderful times. At a round bar table was a burly woman very, very drunk. Everyone at the table was laughing uncontrollably. The burly woman turned to us, and everyone stopped laughing. "Hey Frick, you sweet little tart," the lady said. Frick then closed the page to the memory.

"Xemu," was all he said.

That was Xemu? Xemu was a cross-dressing dude. I went through all of this to party with a cross-dresser. Here I was now, together as one, with a horrible spawn of Satan and my hopeful party bud was into a kind of party that I wasn't really too interested in joining. Space Sucked!

Through the years Frick had forgotten about Xemu. It was I who had brought back that bad glimmering page in the book. Xemu wasn't going to be happy with me either. So much for a grandiose entrance, I thought. Frick was *a frickin'* psychopath - he was going to kill Xemu and everyone he had ever met.

CHAPTER 42

A Croc of a Birthday

Where we had been heading all this time, I hadn't had time to think too much about... Nah, why lie about it? I was traveling in space. I had plenty of time to think about anything. I thought about it alright. I'm telling you it really was on my mind. Just not that much. I probably should have thought about it more. I mean they say it's the journey not the destination, but while up here in space it's all about the destination and not the journey.

After asking a few times, what I had learned was that we were on a path to an orphanage of underage humans. Well, not totally humans but the closest thing to humans in the Milky Way Galaxy. Our mission was to pick up thirty to forty of the little bastards and to then take them to Polysee. Polysee was the king of the planet of crocodiles. The kid humans were meant to be a present to Polysee for his one-hundredth birthday. Once there they'd be stripped down and consumed by Polysee and his high court.

However, now that Frick had been reminded about his vendetta against Xemu, Frick completely abandoned seeing Polysee. Frick had been going to grab the humanlike kids because he was bored. He actually didn't care much for Polysee, and didn't need the "cheese" he'd get from the transaction.

I was trying to find out what the humanlike beings were technically called, but Frick refused to tell me. He said he cared so little it wasn't worth conversing about. "They are such a boring race and even when they age, they are still so dull," he informed me.

Back to "cheese." Currency in space has changed dramatically through the ages. According to Frick, the original medium of currency was females. The problem was that the females quickly became tired of the males and insisted on being traded more often. This caused an influx of trade, and nothing was anyone's for very long at all.

Upon realizing this was a flaw in any currency trading system the females dropped the veil, figuratively, and informed the males that they had in fact been trading the males without their knowledge for some time now. That really stirred the pot because males then came to the realization there had been no currency at all. How long had this been going on? Hundreds of years? Thousands of years? Males were outraged. Females wouldn't answer.

No one ever did find out. However, stopping all trading for a brief time once again aligned the sexes and made for better relationships for many years to come.

Next came the use of paper currency. An elaborate system was devised but became very difficult to manage. Some life forms didn't care what paper was exchanged, but most did. And so, arguments ensued about what a piece of paper ultimately was worth and what it should look like.

In summation, roughly eight to ten thousand years ago paper currency was abolished, and it was agreed upon that a better unit for commerce would be "cheese." All lifeforms loved cheese, but not all loved females, and many lifeforms couldn't read. Cheese had become the victorious winner as a quite perfect currency.

Making the decision to not pick up the children for cheese, we were now headed on a very different mission. Frick and I had both wanted to meet up with Xemu, and we were on the path to doing so. Frack.... Well, she was on no path at all. That little cunt was dead. Tired of seeing her body lying there, I consulted with Frick on what to do with it.

Frick's body cannoned out the garbage chute and into the vast expanse of space. We watched while the body floated farther and farther away until it was gone. "That wasn't very ceremonious Frick. We could have put a sticker on her forehead so passerby's would at least know she was dead. I mean something…"

"We were one," he interrupted me.

In this context, those few now often heard words sounded heartfelt. "That actually sounded nice Frick. Good job big fella," I replied.

"One day that will be you, Steve. Boom. Out the door. Bye." Was Frick's matter-of-fact retort. And then he walked off. "Way to ruin the moment!" I yelled down the corridor.

CHAPTER 43

Married to Frick

Being linked to Frick was weird. I had never used a lot of brain power and now I was being forced to use heaps of it. Thinking all the time was tiring. Being a they/them is not as easy as you'd think. It's tough. Solace came to me in the evenings. When asleep I felt like myself again.

When sleeping I'd think of the good times back on Earth. I thought mostly of Mary Sue. It would be nice to say she was a good person, but I knew she wasn't. Still, she was the closest thing I had ever had to a girlfriend and so I thought about her a lot.

Why was she the closest thing I had ever had to a girlfriend? I'd had time to think about that too, and I probably wasn't the nicest person either. Maybe that is why Frick linked up with me. With all the bad crap he'd done in his life, he'd hardly want to link up with Ghandi. Considering the arguments Ghandi and Frick would have, nothing would ever get done. "Storm the desert!" Frick would yell. Ghandi would reply back, "Why don't we just walk the desert and look for salt?"

It would be a shit show. Was I enough of an asshole for Frick? How long would it take for him to bore of me and to unlink me? Would he dump me off and I'd end up like poor Frack before I even met Xemu? Frack was awful but she sure was a cute little thing. I mean, before she died and got all sucked up that was. When she was spit out the garbage chute, she looked like a shriveled-up raisin monkey. I also wondered if it was just a coincidence that their names sounded so good as one. Barf Candy and Frick didn't have the same ring to it as Frick and Frack. That was the kind of stuff I dreamt about.

When I was awake, Frick and I would constantly bicker. Salt VS sugar, chocolate VS white chocolate, licorice VS Red Vines, pineapple on pizza, is a hot dog a sandwich, and so on. You know important stuff like that. We just couldn't agree on anything. He'd want to share with me murder stories and I'd wish I could play video games on the shuttle. Where was this Blastar game they spoke of? Frick talked so much, and it was always about him. A narcissist who's also a mass murderer is the worst, trust me.

CHAPTER 44

Three's a Crowd

For better or for worse, most of the time worse, we were now on track to see Xemu. All the pieces had aligned together thus far. A few hiccups here and there, sure, but the point was things had come together, and the two of us were now here. And so once again where was here?

I looked out the window. The relaxing monotony of space. Instead of relaxing though it was I who was making it anything but relaxing. I could feel how much Frick despised Xemu. The hatred coursed through my entire body.

I wondered if Frick felt the opposing anticipation of my excitement to meet Xemu. If so, that must have infuriated him. Meeting Xemu would be the culmination of everything I had set out to do. On the other hand, maybe the three of us would work it all out. A sharp pang of hatred surged through my body - Frick had sent it my way. Then again maybe not, I thought.

"You can't do that if I don't get to know what you are so mad about!" I yelled at no one. I knew that fucker could hear me though and I really did know what he was angry about. Why did he hate Xemu so much? Maybe Xemu had played with his little tentacle in the wrong way. It was hard to say.

Elon's starship pushed on through the universe. My brain incessantly running, I was now finding the infinity of space claustrophobic. This of course bothered me because what could be more the exact opposite. Yet here I was, inventing mental problems for myself to hopefully one day get over. The most exciting time of my life, and here I was complicating things. A very human attribute.

I spent my time alone. Weeks went by and we kept moving forward into the unknown. I didn't see Frick much ever. Not that I went looking for him either. There wasn't a need. I didn't like him, and if seeing him was an excuse to make conversation with someone, we could do that anyway.

I thought more about Xemu and why I had chosen to meet him. What was I supposed to say or do with him anyhow? It's not like we could go get beers now. It seemed like I had found his mortal enemy, and I was bringing that enemy right to his front door. Not exactly the way to gain friends. However, without that enemy, I would have never found him. I surmised all these pieces were completing a puzzle and each piece must be meant to be. There was a bigger picture.

I could feel the anger building daily within Frick. I presumed that meant every day we were getting a little closer to the emperor himself.

CHAPTER 45

Crash Handling

I woke up to the ship rocking to and fro and then a loud crash. We had landed somewhere. I ran to the top of the ship and found Frick sitting in the captain's chair. Not saying anything, Frick threw up his tree arms up and left the room. "This thing seriously can't park automatically?" I asked.

Getting out of the ship, we saw that Frick had blown out one of the shuttle's landing legs. The ship lay on the tarmac like an injured dog. "We can get it fixed here, right?" I asked. "What do you think, they let all the broken spacecraft just sit here until someone is able to get rid of them?" Frick replied. I watched on as another ship crash-landed on the tarmac, sliding into our ship. Several drunk aliens tottered out of the spaceship laughing. None of them paid any attention to having crashed into Elon Musk's shuttle. I guess he wasn't liked that much in space either. I followed Frick into the building looking back periodically. The tarmac looked more like a demolition derby than a landing site.

CHAPTER 46

I'm Xemu, Baby

The building was filled with all sorts of alien life forms. The place itself a massive nightclub. Though I wasn't sure if it was still called a nightclub up in space. Here there was no night or day. Maybe they just called it a club. Scantily clad beings of all sorts filled the place where nighttime reigned.

In the far back sitting at a circular booth, the section where patrons of the club actually paid their bills no doubt, sat Xemu. How did I know it was Xemu? Other than the brief glimpse I had had of him through Frick, I knew because he was wearing a large gold chain with big, studded-lettered diamonds. I read the letters aloud to myself. "I'm Xemu, Baby."

Xemu himself was a massive hulk of a human. But looking at him closer, he actually wasn't. He was shaped like a man, but his body parts were all extenuated. They were too big. He had huge bulging eyes, an oversized sniffer, massive sledgehammer-like hands, and yet he had very tiny ears. But then maybe again they weren't that small. Maybe it was just that everything else on him was just that big. Xemu looked odd but somewhat normal all at the same time. Yet what stood out more than anything else was his garb. The Galactic Overlord was indeed, as I had learned, a drag queen.

My first thought – NO FUCKING WAY. My second immediate thought was Xemu must really think about what to wear in the morning. He looked great. I on the other hand had totally told myself I would wear black when meeting him and here I was in a freakin' green U2 shirt. "I really should have spent more money at the Hot Topic," I mumbled to myself. "Damn U2, crappy ass band."

Flanked around Xemu, at the table, sat a group of Caitlyn Jenner lookalikes. I was finally going to meet Xemu, and I didn't have a word to say. I was gobsmacked. I kept looking at those sledgehammer hands. How does a guy with rough hands like that masturbate?

Walking towards the table, my brain raced. Where Frick had wandered off to, I was unsure. I didn't doubt I'd be dealing with that hot mess soon though.

The place itself was huge and loud. It was like heaven's very own Burning Man. As I walked by the bar, I eyeballed all sorts of drunk aliens. Some were passed out on the bar, some were dancing, and one had three heads and used all three to head butt another alien right in front of me, but all the awake aliens... they seemed to be having a good time.

"I'm fucking tell you. I left a whole bag here of cheese curds. I was using them to play billiards. I ain't lying. I put a few in the table to play some pool and then the rest were gone. I want my fucking cheese curds back," an alien was yelling at the bartender. I noted the alien was cussing. That was good because it meant I would fit right in.

"Your drunk ass probably ate all the cheese curds, Gobletlygook," the bartender responded. "I didn't eat shit, I'm allergic to cheese. That's why I'm always broke. I can't even handle the fucking stuff. This is bullshit. I want my cheese back or I'm going to burn this fuckin' place down. Fuck you and fuck everyone in here."

The bartender handed Gobletlygook a drink. "Fine, here drink this. We're even. Complaining about a few cheese curds like it's some big deal or something. You're acting like you lost a whole cheese wheel."

Gobletlygook downed the drink. Instantly, his eyes rolled back into his head, and he passed out on the floor. The aliens all around him found the event hilarious. "Get him out of here!" yelled the bartender. A few security guards picked him up off the floor and dragged Gobletlygook away.

In the far corner, there was an uproarious cheer that took over the moment. A wedding ceremony was taking place, and it looked like the officiant was an Elvis impersonator. Focusing my eyes more and more on Elvis, he sure looked good. I started questioning if it really may actually be him. Was it cooler to meet another human up in a space club, or was it cooler to run into Elvis? It was way cooler to run into Elvis for sure, but I hadn't come to meet Elvis. I turned my efforts back towards Xemu.

I expected none of this, but as I put one step before the other, I had to concentrate on what to say. This was my moment. I hummed the song "One Foot in Front of the Other" from the movie *Revenge of the Nerds.* The song always helped me chill out and focus on moving ahead. "You got to put one foot in front of the other... Got to put one foot in front of the other..."

I stood before Xemu's table, all looked on at me. "U2 is a shitty band, sorry," I said.

Xemu nodded up at me. "I'll take another round for Bruce, Caitlyn..." Xemu stopped for a moment stuck on the next person's name at the table. "Caitlyn, sir," she said. "Right... and Bruce," he said pointing to the last person at the table and then nodding his approval. "Yeah, kiddo another round for all of them," he reiterated.

Xemu thought I was a waiter. I'd been told to never meet your heroes. Still standing in front of them, though admittedly not as proud, I saw Xemu begin to sense I wasn't part of the staff. "Caitlyn's... Bruce's... Up," he declared. Everyone stood up from the table and shuffled out of the way for the great Galactic Overlord. Xemu now stood before me chest to chest. Well, head to pelvis. He was wearing high heels but towered over me regardless. His sequin dress flowed like a great ship's sail. His head, the mast, held high. Frick wouldn't have a hard time finding us. Saying we stood out in the crowd would have been a gross understatement. And it was a statement because everyone in this crowd certainly stood out.

Xemu looked back at the table of Jenners, and then to me. "They are the most beautiful things in the universe, aren't they?" the Overlord earnestly whispered in my ear, his muscled arms and neck bulging in my face. I didn't reply. Bert would have liked these Jenners. The work done on them was perfect. They genuinely all looked like the same person. They were just as plastic surgeons liked.

If Andre the Giant had had muscle definition like Arnold Schwarzenegger, he still wouldn't have been as impressive as Xemu. Xemu reminded me of a Silverback Gorilla but harbored the intensity of a Cape buffalo. You can tell a lot about a person by their eyes. Animals' eyes tell a lot too. The Cape buffalo's eyes are piercing. Unafraid of anything. Unassuming never.

"I find them comfortable," Xemu said. "Huh," I replied. Xemu picked up his dress and was wearing pantyhose underneath. I sure wished at that moment I had been wearing pantyhose as well. I never thought I'd say that. But talk about a way to befriend this particular Overlord. Instead, I had forgotten to pack underwear. Xemu might be the last guy I'd want to know that though.

"I came here from Earth because I wanted to meet you," I told him. "I know," Xemu replied. "You can read minds too?" I asked. "No, everyone wants to meet me," he said. Bored, the Jenners drifted off into the crowd. "Sorry to scare off your Jenners," I said. "I'd like to say it's OK and that there are more of those where they came from. But we both know there are not," he replied.

We should probably figure something out. I don't hide very well," he said. I turned around to see what Xemu was looking at. On the other side of the club, flailing aliens bounced into walls in every direction. A tree arm broke through a window and turned its tip towards Xemu. Frick had found him.

Xemu looked down at me with those penetrating Cape buffalo eyes I was talking about and let out the loudest and longest fart I had ever heard. Aliens scurried in every which way, but all ways away from us. "Now that is what you call a bomb. Not very ladylike but it works every time," he said. Xemu picked me up like a child's doll and made a mad dash toward a back door in the club.

Slamming the back door closed behind us, he dropped me to the floor. He could have been a bit more gracious about it, but I guess being gentle isn't a mascara-wearing Silverback Gorilla's strong suit.

The hallway had rows of doors. Aliens were walking in and out of them washing their hands.

"Where are we?" I asked. "Bathrooms. If you didn't notice I gotta go," he said. "What about Frick?" I asked. "I gotta go. You wait here," he replied.

"We are one. He knows where I'm at Xemu!" I yelled. Xemu had started reading the doors to see which bathroom he could enter. "Frick can't go into a bathroom he's not allowed into. Big deal up here in space," he said. "There are at least twenty types of different signs," I said. "Yep, we are very particular about excrement," Xemu said.

Down the hall Frick ripped the back door off its hinges. "What did you do to this guy?" I asked. "I ate his hamburger," he said while opening the door to a bathroom. "Hamburger?" I asked. "Yeah, we both love them. Now give me a moment," he said. "Is that code for something? You can't be serious," I asked.

Frick's tree arms scrambled the walls back, stopping at where we were stood. I'd seen how that ended last time, and it was time to go. "I don't know what bathroom they have for you. Humans don't come here," Xemu explained to me calmly. I pushed past Xemu, into the bathroom, and closed the massive door behind us.

CHAPTER 47

Just A Couple Guys Hanging Out in the Bathroom

The bathroom stalls were huge. Xemu closed the privacy door to the stall behind him, while I waited by the sinks. "You sure he isn't going to come in here, Xemu?" I asked. "Yep," he replied through the door. I felt like a little kid waiting for my mom to finish up in the bathroom at a department store.

Xemu came out and washed his hands. "No one will ever say Xemu is not hygienic," he said. "So, here's the problem. We are connected. He knows exactly where I'm at." I began to explain to him.

"Well, yeah. He saw us walk in here too. I'm sure that helped," Xemu said while drying his hands on massive paper towels. "Is anyone going to come in here?" I asked. "Doubtful. My kind are rare in this galaxy." Xemu pulled out a make-up kit and began to apply mascara around his huge eyes. I paced back and forth behind him.

"We cannot go back out that door. I don't want to be connected to this guy, and I don't think there is anything I can do about it. I saw him kill the last alien person thing like nothing when he disconnected from her to connect to me. I came all the fucking way up here to party with you, and now that I know how you party, the last thing I want to do is party with you. That's not my kind of party!" While I ranted on, I came to realize who I was speaking to. With that in mind, I lowered my voice a notch, "I mean not to be rude."

"No, not rude at all. The price of lipstick has gone up

astronomically. Have you noticed that on your planet too?" The Warlord asked changing the subject. "I don't know," I politely responded. "Can you climb into that first stall and turn the water off at the toilet for me please?" he asked.

Perplexed, I walked into the bathroom and crouched down between the oversized toilet and the stall wall. Was this a ploy for Xenu to kill me? Maybe I had gone too far? "I don't hear it running," I said as I turned the valve off. Xemu didn't reply. I came back out of the stall and stood next to him once again.

"I'm a problem solver young man. That's how I'd like people to think of me," he said while putting his makeup back into a pink-tinted transparent makeup bag. "That's funny because I was just saying how I am not really a problem solver," I said. Xemu strolled back into the stall and ripped the toilet right from the base out of the floor. Water sprayed like a geyser everywhere.

"I thought that would work. I guess not." He nonchalantly looked at me. "Oh, well" is all he said. The bathroom was now flooding fast.

"Up or down," he asked me through the thunder of rushing water. "I mean up. I flew all the way up here in the first place and now I'm not even sure what the hell...." Stopping mid-sentence, I watched on as Xemu began to rip at the roof of the bathroom.

"Why don't you break down one of the walls?" I yelled over the sound of gushing water. "Can't take that chance. Remember very bad to use a bathroom here you are not supposed to use." He yelled back at me. "The alternative is to die in here," I pled. "Can't do it," the Warlord replied.

The room sealed tight; it didn't take long for the bathroom to fill entirely with water. We soon found ourselves at the top of the room kissing the ceiling and both gasping for air. Xemu had picked the wrong bathroom door to go through. We were going to die – trapped in an alien lavatory.

CHAPTER 48

A Poop Party

In a great crash, the floor of the bathroom caved, and a thousand gallons of water dumped below bringing Xemu and me down with it. Water doesn't break a two-story fall, but something wonderful did. Whatever I had landed on was soft. I had settled on what felt like a plume of cotton candy. And the smell... The smell was amazing. Had I fallen into a sweets factory? I don't think I have ever felt more comfortable in my life. I closed my eyes and took in all of what this wonderful place had to offer. Content in my comfortable cocoon, a large hand reached down, grabbed onto my index finger, and pulled me out of my personal haven.

"We need to get out of here," Xemu whispered. "In a little bit - this place is great," I replied. I again intoxicated myself by inhaling as much dreamy air as my lungs could handle. What a far cry from the scary air on Earth. "As a kid, I dreamt of growing up in a candy store. They have candy stores up here in space Xemu?" I asked.

"You are standing in a pile of excrement," he clarified. Preoccupied with something else, Xemu looked very concerned. "Oh, man." I picked up my hand and extended my index finger. "You pulled my finger, Xemu," I laughed aloud. I was so proud. Xemu stared on at me ignoring my finger held high. It took me a moment to notice, but he wasn't staring at me at all but rather through me.

Slowly turning around, a large mushy amorphous face was but a few inches away from my nose. Whoever owned this face looked like an oozing marshmallow. The eyes of the creature stared intensely into mine. "You sure smell nice fella, but you are clearly in my personal space right now," I told it. "That is no fella, and I can assure you she's not going to like what you just said," Xemu whispered.

Offended, the large face, attached to a giraffe-like neck, whipped back. "Nude, rude, crude, handsome dude," she said. Clearly embarrassed, she hurriedly pulled her underwear back up her legs, pushing the gelatinous fat out of the way. Terrified, she then fluffed her dress back down to her ankles, and nowhere else to go, pushed her way off to the corner of the room. "Oh God, and she's royalty too," Xemu said.

I felt bad for her and watched on as her dress bubbled and swayed back and forth. The dress was made of a plastic material and had two functions. One, an important part in all dresses, was to look pretty. The second function was reserved more for the practicality of retaining all of the goo her body was made up of. "She's an Allinav. They only eat sweets. They aren't so sweet though," Xemu informed me.

"Wow," was all I could think of to add to the conversation. Xemu continued, "This is really bad. Only Allinav women of royal lineage speak in rhymes kiddo. This is not a good situation."

"She's royalty and that is the best she could rhyme. They must have awful schooling up here," I said.

"She's young. They get better in time," Xemu informed me.

"Well, me no worry in a hurry but maybe you and me Xemu should... scurry," I rhymed back.

"It's just the women who rhyme Steve. Just the women," Xemu corrected me.

Seeing the door and the circular motif on it, I realized Xemu was right: we were in another bathroom. "We're in the..." Xemu interrupted me. "Yes, we are in an Allinav bathroom and that must be the daughter of the overseer of this entire floating establishment. I think we're in the royal private quarters," Xemu informed me.

"And just what is the penalty for being in the wrong bathroom anyway, Xemu? I mean really who cares?" I asked. "Death," he bluntly replied.

"Oh," was all I said. That changed things up a bit. I didn't realize this was all that serious. "You know what they say, a little death never hurt anybody," I said to try and chill things out a bit. Xemu didn't acknowledge the comment.

The bathroom door opened and a still embarrassed Allinav, now I knew of royal descent, scurried out of the room. For a moment nothing happened. We both waited to see who was going to come through the empty door next.

CHAPTER 49

That is a Tasty Burger

In through the door walked Frick. "Could be worse," Xemu said. "How's that?" I asked. "If it were another Allinav, we'd already be dead," Xemu said.

A tree arm whipped across the room and slowly coiled around Xemu's neck. Like a Boa constrictor, it tightened and then tightened again. "Now maybe we have ten minutes or so," Xemu said while choking.

The great hulk of Xemu was easily picked up from the ground. "This is all over a hamburger?" I exclaimed to no one in particular.

I knew Frick was into food. But through all that time in space, he had never once thought of hamburgers. It made a bit of sense he would like them though, even Vegetarians had tried to copy hamburgers with those grass burgers they ate. I mean everyone likes hamburgers.

The laser from an alien gun cut through the air and burned into Frick's arm. The arm withdrew in pain dropping Xemu back into the mass of candy Allinav shit. Rushing in came the they/them of the Bruce Caitlyn Jenners and standing like the glorious women of the show Charlie's Angels they/them began shooting their love guns everywhere throughout the room, but that wasn't all. As each bullet fired sparklers and glitter streamed through the air. It was all magical. The Jenners had come to save the day. While each love gun was emblazoned with the word "love," the bullets themselves... they meant business, and Frick was forced to cower back in pain to a lone corner of the room.

Frick smirked. Still connected as one, Frick turned to me and shared all the pain he was going through in the moment. I fell to my knees and clutched my arm in agonizing pain.

Into the bathroom marched a small group of Allinav soldiers. "Who dare disgrace me, entering an Allinav latrine on my vessel? A royal latrine! You have violated the chastity of my wife and for that crime, you are ALL sentenced to death."

One of the Caitlyn Jenners looked at another Caitlyn, or possibly a Bruce, and spoke.

"Well, Fuck."

I had the same thought as they did. I mean them did. Either way, the Jenners had once again said all there really was that needed to be said. Nonetheless, I felt compelled to say something too.

"This all reminds me of the time I had met a guy at the bar, Caitlyn Bruce. We had totally become drinking buds and were hanging out all the time. It was great. And even though we always had fun, he kept telling me how I should really meet his wife one day, and then we could all hang out together. The guy totally loved her. Well, finally one day it happened. I met the wife, and while I know this sounds like a swinger story, that's not what ended up going down, Caitlyn Bruce.

Sure enough, I had slept with the guy's wife years earlier. It was super awkward, and you know what, Bruce Caitlyn? That time I thought I was gonna die too. But I didn't die. I did lose a drinking pal though. And I don't want to be insincere about it all, so I'll be honest with you. It was worth it. It was fucking worth it! She had been great man, or woman/man, or whatever you want to call yourself, but, yes there is a but, I still missed my drinking friend afterwards. Maybe after all this, you can be my new drinking friend bro/lady Caitlyn Jenner." I couldn't help reflecting on the story still. "Man, she sure was a hell of a woman, Bruce. Hell of a woman."

I would never get my answer from Jenner. Each of us was manhandled and ushered out of the room.

CHAPTER 50

An Earth Man in Alcatraz

I sat in my own cell, resolute I was to die alone. I did my best to focus on my drinking friend's wife because that made me happy, but my present situation was just too bad. It wasn't working. My biggest fear in life thus far was that I'd die watching some weird freaky midget porn or something like that; holding my cock in one hand and a My Little Pony doll in the other. Now, I love My Little Pony - just to clarify, there is nothing weird about the My Little Pony part just the freaky midget porn part. Oh, and don't worry it would have definitely been American-made weird midget porn. It still wouldn't have been some foreign-made weird porn shit. I will never change my mind on that. My concern was that the firefighters who found me dead would think I watched that weird stuff all the time and would think I was a weirdo. I was only a weirdo when I got really bored. Oh, the firefighters... Sorry, let me explain the firefighters - they would be there because I probably would have set my ball hair on fire knowing I was dying. Anyhow, the firefighters would think I was a weirdo all the time, and not just when I was bored, and my legacy would all be a lie. A tainted fallacy of the essence of who I really was as a man.

Frick made no attempt to contact me, nor I him. Food came once a day. And every day like clockwork, I heard someone walk by humming the awful song ninety-nine bottles of beer on the wall. Those routine beer countdowns were my only gauge of how many days I had been there. I figured that I had been there a total of one day and three-quarters when the door opened.

The light hurt my eyes, and I cowered back into a corner.

Crouched down, I covered my face. My time had come. If you think you have a full mental image of the disarray of this scene, you probably don't. I can't possibly paint the full picture here. I was feeling pain mixed in with pockets of shock and despair with some self-pity sprinkled in between a rainbow of emotions. I was an impressionist painter with only traditional colors left on my palette. I had walked a different walk, and it had been a hell of a journey but now the journey had come to an end. Frankly, I hadn't been beat. It was worse. I was tired, burned out.

Feeling a long gluttonous finger under my chin, my head was gently lifted back up. Once again, I fought to look into the light. Before me stood an Allinav woman in a flowing dress. As the dress undulated up and down her sweet, wonderful smells began to fill my cell. The Allinav beauty had either farted, or she didn't wipe when done. Either way, that wonderful smell rejuvenated me with a little bit of life once again. Whatever would happen next, I would appreciate this moment.

Holding me by the hand, I was marched through several hallways and into a changing room. The Allinav woman handed me a G-String with a fabric elephant trunk attached to it, and without a word, left the room.

It was apparent that I was supposed to put them on, so I promptly disrobed with the speed I'd use at a doctor's appointment and then proceeded to fold my clothes nicely on the bench. My willie now snug in the elephant trunk and my butt cheeks flapping in the air conditioning, I waited. That is right I waited not wafted. OK, the truth is I wafted, and I waited. I was sure why I had wafted. I wafted regularly and maybe that is why these Allinavs and I seemed to get along well. However, I wasn't sure what I was "waiting" for. Looking at myself in a mirror I was sure something fun was no doubt about to go down.

My ass looked pretty good in that mirror. I had always been a butt guy. I think it was because as a kid those My Little Pony dolls' asses sure did smell good. Adult asses not so much - but either way I think that is what made me a butt guy. Strawberry Shortcake dolls' hair sure smelled good too. I wondered why I thought about My Little Pony asses first. Strawberry Shortcake dolls were actually cute. Instead, I thought of a horse's ass? If I ever made it back to Earth, I'd go to one of those My Little Pony conventions and see if the guys there all were smelling the asses too. I'd bet none of the guys at those Brony conventions are boob guys.

My thoughts were interrupted, one of the double doors flew open and dozens of Allinav children burst into the room while gorging on sweets. I never understood why people locked one door when there was a pair of double doors. They should either be both locked or both unlocked. It made no sense, and yet people do it all the time. I guess aliens did it all the time too.

Once all in the room, we stood opposite one another in dead silence. The moment only lasted just that, because quickly uninterested, the children continued to gorge on their sweets ignoring me while I stood still watching on.

Next, the Allinav woman who had freed me from my solitary confinement walked into the room. "You idiot. That was supposed to go on your face. You are meant to be a clown. It is the emperor's son's birthday. What did you think you were going to be doing?" she said to me abruptly rushing me out of the room. All the while the children remained completely disinterested.

"Oh, I would have made a pretty poor clown with my dangly bits dancing around," I answered her.

CHAPTER 51

I've Done Worse

The room she hurried me into was a grand suite. It was once again filled with that euphoric, wonderful, sweet smell, and the scene was complimented by wall-to-wall red velvet. I stood there in my elephant G-string and waited for something to happen next. If Xemu was still alive I sure hoped it wouldn't involve him because I wouldn't want this situation to get awkward.

In walked in what must have been the emperor's wife. "Yep," I said while shaking my head positively. I had no idea what to say. She wore the same flowing dress attire I had seen on the other Allinav women but was additionally adorned with heaps of jewelry. I say heaps because none of the jewelry was light or delicate. It was garish. It was as if Mr. T had been her personal jewelry shopper.

"Come on, come over here. Oh, young lad, please bring your body near. For I am in need, and you are indeed, delightful," she said to me lying out on the bed. Much like her, the bed was massive. I'd say it was the size of two king-size beds pushed together. I walked over and as requested; I rested my loins next to hers.

The smell... Oh, the smell... I was truly intoxicated once again with the fantastic smell of sweets. It must be like how a heroin addict feels when scoring smack.

I knew what she wanted. I had been through that harem house with Mary Sue. I knew what this room was built for.

What happened next may surprise you, or at this point maybe not. Either way, it is what happened. Closing my eyes, my elephant buried deep… real deep… in what can only be described as layers of gelatinous sweet royal love folds.

I never did open my eyes, but at some point, I fell asleep. Waking up with an ear-to-ear smile, one of the Jenners stood above me. "Shhh," they/them/she whispered.

Now I have to be honest. I really wouldn't have wanted anyone to know what I had just done. Especially the emperor who had made it clear he thought I had already defiled his daughter. If he thought that I defiled his daughter, I can't even imagine his thoughts on what I did to his wife.

"Yeah, baby!" I said to myself laughing. I had hoped I was thinking it loud enough that Frick heard too. "I fucked an alien empress goo creature, Frick. You asshole." Not a very adult response but I felt it was the necessary thing to do.

Waking up from lovemaking and looking a Bruce/ Kaitlyn Jenner in the eyes should really not be on anyone's love list. "Here put these on," they/them/she/he said.

"Are you Bruce or Caitlyn?" I asked. "I'm Bruce." He/she/they/ them said. "Oh, good," I replied. Not quite sure why it mattered but it made me feel better knowing, nonetheless.

Bruce handed me my pants and my shirt. I quickly put them on, leaving my elephant appendage on the floor. It wasn't the first time I'd had a one-night stand, and I sure hoped it wouldn't be my last. I felt like a rock star. I still had it!

CHAPTER 52

Bruce, The F1 Driver

In the hallway Bruce had a small commuter spaceship all ready to get us out of there. Bruce jumped into the driver's seat and I into the passenger. "Let's do this!" Bruce yelled out.

"Bruce, you are way too excited. We are not out of this yet, and you do not exactly have the best driving record you know," I said.

"Son, I take offense to that. You wanted a drinking partner? That is not the kind of attitude that is going to get you one." Bruce still in the driver's seat, we took off down the corridor to freedom.

Bruce tore through the place. "You sure know your way around here pretty good!" I yelled over the roar of the engines. "I grew up here!" Bruce yelled back. Pedal to the metal, down the final stretch, the sky opened up before us, and we found ourselves on the tarmac next to some strewn-out dead alien body. Bruce killed the engines and all we could hear was the dead alien snoring loudly. I guess he wasn't dead after all. Stepping over the alien it was none other than Gobletlygook. Still in a rush, Bruce and I made our way towards Elon's shuttle.

"Sorry to have doubted you, Bruce," I said. "No fucking problem. Don't forget to eat your Wheaties little bro," he/she/them/their/ person of interest said.

Xemu stood at the top of the steps to board the ship. Bruce patted me on the ass. "Get on the ship you sick fuck."

"OK, the moment is over," I said, trying to put an end to all this bonding affectionate crap between Bruce and I.

I did owe an explanation to Xemu though. "You don't understand... the smell... It was wonder..." I tried to explain but was cut off.

"I wouldn't recommend staying here Bruce," Xemu said. It was true. What they had to talk about was infinitely more important than anything I had to say. I walked up into the mouth of the shuttle. I would let them figure out who was going where. However, I wanted to make sure I was one of the ones leaving this place. It's not a good idea to have sexy time with some royal alien guy's obese Mr. T-looking wife and then hang out to play checkers afterwards.

"I just banged an alien," I said while nodding approval. The nod was for no one but myself. I wasn't expecting anyone to answer me either. I was just proud of myself. Uninterested in my sexual exploits, Xemu looked at me and then back to Bruce.

"I don't know where else to go anymore my friend. I've tried so many places and never felt how I want to feel in any of them," Bruce said.

"I understand. I really do." Xemu picked his necklace up from his mighty chest and held it up high. "Sometimes I don't even think my name is Xemu. Something close perhaps, but not Xemu."

Bruce closed his/her/they/them's eyes and raised his/her/they/them/their arms to the skies. From the club door, ran the three other Jenners, and chaos reigned behind themshehim. Siren's blaring, gun-yielding aliens emptied from the club, bullets airborne everywhere.

"It's time to go," Xemu told me. I put both my arms down by my sides and air fucked my alien. "It's like air guitar but it's air banging," I explained myself to Xemu.

Xemu and I watched on as a flood of bullets hit the Jenners. They/them/he/she's determination never waned and as all three of the

Jenners moved onward toward us I watched on in awe. Surely, no Olympic games could have been this thrilling.

One by one each Jenner collapsed into Bruce, each one more hurt than the other. It's not good to come in last in a race. I don't mean they bumped into he/she/they?them either. They literally ran into Bruce's center... Bruce's being... Bruce's inner chi... Bruce's chakra... They/them/their/he/she became one. Now an IT.

All bullets now deflected off of IT. Xemu, the aliens, and I watched in awe as each Jenner united to become one larger and larger mass of pureed energy. A puree of Hollywood stars with Bruce standing front and center. I say Hollywood stars because I realized in that moment that this Bruce/Caitlyn thing was a puree of all of Hollywood. And what had happened was Hollywood had saved us. The puree wasn't the Kardashians, Paris Hilton, Kanye, OJ Simpson, or Britney Spears, but at the same time, IT was. The Hollywood tabloid celebrities had come together to save me/I.

Once merged, the lone Jenner, the last Jenner, lit up like a Volkswagen magnesium engine block set on fire. The flash of light was blinding, and while it kept intensely growing for the second time that day, I had to turn away.

Screaming up to the sky, Bruce yelled out, "Goonies never say die." I forced myself to once again look at Bruce. I loved that movie too and I understood where Bruce was coming from. I nodded my approval and a tear came to my eye. "I'm not crazy," I said to Xemu for what he seemed to feel was for no apparent reason. But I had reason. Oh, I had plenty of reason. Light and energy poured from every Jenner orifice. And then came the blast. A blast of energy that was deafening. Like an atom bomb, it struck in all directions and mowed down every alien on the deck.

"The most beautiful thing in the universe," I said. "Yep," agreed Xemu.

A new army of alien warriors emerged from the club. In the

center of them all was a severely charred Frick. Collectively hurried, Xemu spoke to Bruce, "Come my love. You, me, and Barf Candy all have one thing in common. None of us have felt at peace anywhere. Come with us once again and let's find peace somewhere. Somewhere over the rainbow, I assure you, skies are blue. And the dreams that you dare to dream really do come true."

I was certain I had heard that somewhere else before, but I couldn't quite put my finger on where. Xemu outstretched his massive hand to the being that had once been the Jenners. The puree of non-cerebral or celebrity energy, depending on how you looked at it, formed a second hand. I watched as Xemu's and they/them/their hands embraced. "Wait. How did I get included in this rainbow of life place?" I asked. No one, or nothing, depending on how you looked at it, answered me.

The cloud of light energy was last to board the ship, and the hatch gently closed behind all of us.

"I've taken care of Frick for now," Xemu said. The two of us strapped in, and the engines roared. "Drink this," Xemu said to me, handing me a vial of clear liquid.

I did. I drank it. It was vile.

CHAPTER 53

There's Something About Mary

Waking up, we were floating through space. I wasn't able to decipher much more. All sounds were muted. All colors merged. I was at a complete disconnect from where I was.

Xemu, seeing I was awake came over to me. "You, OK?" he asked.

"I'm fucked up," I replied. At least I think I replied. I wasn't certain if I had said that aloud or not. Xemu poured another vile of the clear substance down my throat and I passed out again.

Waking up a second time I was still a mess.

"Hey there, Pumpkin," Mary Sue said. I closed my eyes and opened them again. "Mary Sue? What the hell are you doing here?" I asked. Xemu came over to the chair I was sitting in. "No, that's still Bruce. We thought you'd like to see someone you care about when you wake up," he said. "It would make you more comfortable," Mary Sue said smiling.

"Mmm. Thoughtful Mary Jane," I murmured back. Maybe that was the purpose of me living this story. To see if Mary Sue and I were meant for one another.

"I thought her name was Mary Sue. It's Mary Jane?" Mary Sue, who was really Bruce, interrupted me. "I'll just call you they/them and leave it at that," I said. "Oh, I like that. Yeah, that works," They/them replied. I looked on as they/them continued to ponder it over. "I do like he/she sometimes though," They/them replied. "Oh, well. No take backsies!" I answered.

I was seeing trails everywhere. "What the hell did you they/themers give me?" I asked. "LSD," Mary Sue replied. "Whoa," I didn't say anything else for a moment. I had set my focus on Mary Sue's breasts. Following my gaze, they/them looked down at them too. "You know when they cremate you your breast implants don't burn up. They kind of just hang out there in the cremation chamber. They have to scoop them up," Mary Sue said.

Xemu interrupted, ready to change the subject. "We had to disconnect you from Frick. He may not like you more than he doesn't like me now, but you my friend are disconnected, and he has no clue where we now are," Xemu informed me while flying the shuttle into nothingness.

"If that's the case, how did Frick know you were at that club that day?" I asked. "I mean, I always go there. It's my spot," Xemu replied. "We traveled months through space on a whim," I asked no one in particular.

"Oh, kind of something fun you missed while sleeping. Bruce here was kind enough to inform me he/she set Frick on fire in his jail cell," Xemu informed me. "Oh, it was nothing, sweetie," Mary Sue said while blushing. "Nothing? I saw him out there on the deck. All burned up and worthless. I would hardly call that nothing, Bruce. Accolades where accolades are due," Xemu replied admiringly.

"Can we agree to either call this energy puree IT thing either Bruce or Mary Sue for now? This is getting very confusing," I chimed in. "How about Mary Bruce," Mary Sue suggested. No one replied and we flew on, the problem possibly resolved.

"Where we off to anyhow?" I asked. Xemu was quick to reply. "Right now, nowhere. You got any suggestions let me know."

"I'm not from around here. Last time I did acid though I smoked some weed after. That would be nice," I said.

"I know a planet of weed. No one ever goes there," Xemu replied. "No one smokes weed in space?" I asked. "No. Not really," he replied. "Any reason why?" I prodded on. Xemu and Mary Sue looked at each other. "No clue," they both said.

"So, the entire planet is weed?" I asked keenly. "Yeah, I think so," Mary Sue replied. "Who owns this planet?" I asked. "I don't think anyone," Xemu replied. "Oh, someone must," Mary Sue said.

"If there is one thing, I've been good at in life it's selling weed. Take me to this planet," I proclaimed. "Aliens aren't going to smoke weed, kid," Xemu laughed. "It smells bad and it's dirty," Mary Sue chimed in. "Take me there!" I repeated excitedly.

"OK, if you say so," Xemu said.

"Oh, I'm always up for a challenge," I replied in my best sneaky voice.

"Did you really think I'd look like Jeff Bezos," Xemu asked me.

The ship turned south, or maybe it was north I had no idea, but we were on our way.

ABOUT THE AUTHOR

Joel Miller

Joel A. Miller is a British-American writer and filmmaker. He is the writer and director of the film The Still Life and wrote the autobiography Memoir of a Roadie.

BOOKS BY THIS AUTHOR

Memoir Of A Roadie

Joel Miller is an ex- roadie for Guns N' Roses, Poison, Stone Temple Pilots, & The Cranberries. The book is an often-hilarious personal account of a young man in his early 20's trying to be a "good" roadie while also trying to understand life's big picture. Through the advice of rock stars and career roadies Joel tries to find the pathway to roadie righteousness.